Loose Livers and Floatin' Kidneys

by
Wayne Ates

ISBN # 0-8059-4111-8
Printed in the United States of America

Contents

Introduction

Public speaking has been my profession most of my adult life. It has seldom frightened me to speak to an audience, but speaking publicly and writing a book are as different as a mouse and a turnip. When I speak publicly, perhaps I should get shaky knees and a dry mouth and sweaty palms and heart palpitations, but I don't. There is no secret known to me as to why I don't; I just don't. Writing, however, is a different story.

A friend asked me, "Have you read a good book lately?"

I said, "No, but I think I'll try writing one."

This book might not be *good*, but it is different from anything I've seen. I've looked all over the place trying to find a book like this one, but I haven't found it, so I concluded that if there was going to be one like this out there, I had to put it out there. "If you want something done right, do it yourself," the saying goes. At least I can get the *do it yourself* part. Whether it's *right*, we'll have to wait and see.

If you read this book, you will be wiser. If you practice it, you will be happier.

Mama had gone shopping. Daddy and I were eating lunch at home. There were two pieces of meat on a plate on the table. One piece of meat was somewhat larger than the other. I put the larger piece on my plate.

My daddy said, "If I had taken a piece of meat before you did, I wouldn't have got the big piece."

I said, "I know you wouldn't have; that's why I went ahead and took it."

Apparently no one else wanted to write the kind of book I wanted to write, so I decided to go ahead and do it.

Many people have asked me to write a book. It just seemed like the appropriate and natural thing for me to do, and I just wanted to see if I could. I wanted, furthermore, to write something that would be down-to-earth, simple, and interesting. I wanted something that would be worthwhile and something that would be read and appreciated by ordinary people. I am one of the most ordinary people you will ever see or hear of, and I just wanted to reach out to my kind of folks. Of course, you high-class folks are welcome to read, too.

I spoke during a meeting in Las Vegas two years ago. As I was leaving the airport on my way to the hotel where the meeting would take place, the guy driving the taxi said, "In town for some shows, gambling, or what?"

I said, "Gotta speak to a group of salespeople in the morning."

"Whatcha gonna speak about?" he asked.

I told him a few things that I might say if I didn't forget them. I didn't know for sure what to tell him, but I said something.

He listened politely, and then he said, "Sounds like common sense to me."

The more I thought about what he said, the more it gripped my mind. *Common sense. It's so rare it has become interesting*, I thought. It has a captivating quality about it, doesn't it? Isn't that amazing? It's so unusual, folks *crave* it. They will *listen* to it. They *absorb* it. They *love* it. They *appreciate* it.

This book is common sense. It is not a plan, a formula, a program, or a strategy. It contains no systems, no models, no techniques, no schedules, no checklists, no charts, no printouts, and no performance evaluations. It is observation and common sense comment. It's a book about excellence in living life. That's the most direct and definitive way I know how to characterize it.

As you read, please let your hair down and have a good time. My hope is that what I have written will encourage you to become less and less of what you shouldn't be and more and more of what you should be.

In my life there is a great deal of room for intellectual, emotional, moral, and spiritual development; therefore, I am fully aware that what is written in these pages is subject to disagreement, to correction, to deletion, to addition, or to further review. It would be highly presumptuous of me not to say so, wouldn't it? I can give you only what I know. It might not be correct. It might not be much, but it's all I've got. For me to attempt to do more would be mighty dumb of me; for me to attempt to do less would be mighty dishonest of me, and neither of those conditions appeals to me.

When I was teaching high school students, one of them nodded in class one day. I said to him, "You cannot sleep in my class."

He said, "I could if you didn't talk so loud."

To you, reader, I say, "I'll try to write loud."

When I started on this book adventure thing, I pondered on a title. I thought of a story I heard years ago, and from that came the title.

On the last night of a revival meeting in a little country church, the guest preacher, standing at the front door of the church, was shaking hands with the people as they were leaving after the service. A lady said to the preacher as she was shaking his hand, "I have really enjoyed your preaching this week, but there's one thing I need to mention to you. All week long you have preached about loose livers, and you ain't said nothin' about people like me who have floatin' kidneys."

"Loose Livers and Floatin' Kidneys." Now there's a book title if I ever heard one. Sort of grabs you, doesn't it?

All of us are livers of life. The point of this book is that we should want to be *good* livers, not *loose* ones. What kinds of things are true of the good livers? You and I will try to hunt up some answers to that question. Well, to complete, we have to commence; so, let's get on with it.

There *are* better ways to a better way. Let's see if we can identify some of them. Stay with me all the way to the end, please. It won't take long. Thanks. I sure do appreciate it.

Oh, one more thing. I'm from the South, so the language in this book reflects that. It's natural and habitual for me to use colloquialisms and other sorts of language informalities when I speak. I don't do otherwise when I write. You and I ought to be as comfortable as possible as we go through this thing. Comfort, then style. Hope you don't mind.

At a post office the other day, I asked a gentleman who walked toward me, "How you doin'?"

He said with a smile, "Oh, I'm workin' on it."

His reply to me was about all I thought of for the rest of the day. The more I think about it even now, the more I like it. *I'm workin' on it.*

I hope that from now on, each and every day that you live, you can truthfully say in terms of living your life excellently, "I'm workin' on it."

Life is Laughing

A man was riding his horse across a creek. The horse became entangled in some roots on the bank, and he began jerking his legs furiously, trying as best he could to get loose from the hold the roots had on him.

Due to the sudden movements of the horse, the rider's foot came out of one of the stirrups, and one of the horse's hooves landed in the stirrup. The rider then said to the horse, "If you're gonna get on, I'm gonna get off."

In our hectic, stress-filled way of life, we need to "get off" more often and have a good laugh at ourselves and at situations. Laughing is a special thing we humans do; we just need to do it more often, for laughter is to the soul what sunshine and rain are to the flowers; it is what oxygen is to the blood.

We can giggle. We can chuckle. We can laugh politely. We can laugh sidesplittingly. We can laugh happily or incredulously. We can laugh loudly or softly.

However we do it, we *can* do it. It's a wonderful gift we have, and there must be special and good reasons for it.

I have met folks who claim they laugh only on the inside, being unable to express anything externally. That's difficult for me to imagine and even more difficult for me to do. If it's funny to me, I have to laugh. I can't keep it inside. I'm afraid to suppress a laugh, for it might go down and hurt something I need. If I laugh till I cry, it should be because something is funny, not because I have ruptured myself.

Laughs, like people, have their own personalities. They are unique in style, sound, intensity, and duration.

When I'm speaking to a group, I try to identify the bellylaugher, the one to whom virtually everything is funny and who is not reluctant to let the laughs roll. Other folks laugh with that person because the laugh is good, and it, within itself, is funny. The bellylaughers will help me get the rest of the audience going. Sometimes a laugh from a good laugher is funnier than what I am saying. That, of course, happens often. Thank goodness for the good laughers! They make my job much easier and a lot more fun. Come to think of it, I wouldn't have a job if people wouldn't or couldn't laugh. Thank God for the lighthearted folks. I wish there were more of them.

Central to the totality of life is a healthy, appropriate sense of humor. It's a great quality to have at home, on the job, at school, at the store, at the bank, at the beauty shop, anywhere, even at church. Healthy humor is never inappropriate.

A healthy sense of humor is good stuff for you emotionally, physically, mentally, and spiritually. Folks who laugh for no reason or for the wrong reason have a problem. That's why I say one's sense of humor ought to be healthy and appropriate.

Humor ought never to offend one's dignity, yours or anyone else's. It should never be used at the expense of the respect we have for ourselves or for others. One's dignity and self-respect are not good targets for a humorous assault. *Healthy* and *appropriate* are the key words applying to the role of humor in our lives.

We need to live life harmoniously, blending many elements in an appropriate, fitting manner. It takes a lot of threads to make the tapestry beautiful. One of those threads is the ability to see, to appreciate, and to lay hold of the tremendous value of healthy humor. The ability to laugh or to appreciate a humorous perspective is one of the most precious gifts with which we humans are endowed. We ought to make the most of that gift, for, without it, other life essentials become disjointed and out of tune.

Several health care professionals have discussed with me the value of a healthy sense of humor in terms of good emotional and physical health. They tell me that healthy humor is beneficial in preventing and in curing certain kinds of illnesses, and in cases in which prevention or cure is impossible, humor is a valuable tool helping patients to cope with their problems. One physician told me, "It's difficult to laugh well without being well." A doctor who thinks like that is special. Not a bad play on words either, doc. Another M.D. said, "Laughing and worry can't function simultaneously." Still another one said, "Bitterness and healthy laughter don't mix well." Those doctors are exactly right.

Humor is one of the things in life that we don't have to understand to enjoy. Most people don't understand electricity or gravity, but they surely do like what those things do. I don't understand humor, what it is, how it works; nevertheless, I know that it is extremely helpful. It helps us to adjust to life's rough spots. It's one of the finest coping devices we have. *How* it works doesn't matter. What matters immensely is that it *does* work.

My ability to back away and view my life from a humorous perspective has helped me deal with difficulties which otherwise would have crushed me like a piece of thin glass under an elephant's foot. It has helped me keep my balance.

It is not now nor has it ever been my intent to play down the importance of regarding the serious seriously, but it is a *real* mistake for one to take *every* circumstance in life seriously. You and I need balance, and humor is indispensable in providing it.

Folks who take themselves seriously are hilariously funny to me. So are the "puttin' on" kind. It tickles me to be around people who consider themselves too important to have a good laugh either at themselves or at situations that obviously have humorous content. I don't know exactly what's going on with them, but something in them precludes their appreciation for the humorous. They don't have time for levity. If only they knew how funny they are. It's not that they try to be. Far from it. It just works out that way.

I can't possibly be impolite and laugh at the airs they put on while I am in their presence, but as soon as I can get away from them, a good laughing spell comes on me. They would have a fit if they knew about that, wouldn't they? Oh well. How much more fun it would have been for all of us if they had come down off that high horse, and we could have had some good, appropriate laughs together.

People who don't pause for a chuckle or for a deep down laugh are missing one of life's most wonderful dimensions. Nothing can take the place of a healthy sense of humor. *Everything* that comes along in life doesn't have to be dealt with. Everything is not big stuff, bottom line stuff, threatening stuff, where-the-rubber-meets-the-road stuff. It's not *all* seriousness, for goodness sake.

Don A. Cooper, Jr. of Columbus, Georgia, said, "You should not be afraid to look foolish now and then. One wouldn't want it to happen too often, but if it happens every once in a while, don't let it bother you. Don't take yourself so seriously."

That's good advice. How much happier all of us would be if we were more like that. Reckon we'll ever get the message?

When I was in college, I told one of my professors in the Department of Education; "You should teach sex education in one of the high schools."

He brightened up, smiled, and said, "You really think so?"

I said, "Yes, sir. You would make the subject so dull the students would have no more interest in it."

For some reason, he didn't see any humor in my comment. I'll bet you did though, even if you are an education professor.

At a meeting attended mostly by municipal officials, special guests were introduced by the master of ceremonies. When he introduced the mayor, he said, "*There* is what happened because the people of our city did not vote."

The mayor smiled a little, but I had the feeling he thought that comment wasn't all that funny; however, it was hilarious to everybody else who was there.

My niece Kim and her husband Benny live in Jesup, Georgia. Benny asked Kim if she would go to the store and get him a jockstrap. Kim said, "They don't sell jockstraps in the petite size."

The last I heard about the deal, Benny still hadn't laughed.

After listening respectfully to a preacher struggle through a rather dull sermon, I said to him, "I noticed you preached without using any notes."

He smiled proudly and said, "Yeah, I just preached out of my head."

I said, "Sure sounded like it."

He expressed no sense of humor.

While speaking to a group of football coaches a while ago, I said, "I've been in the audiences on some occasions when some of you were doing the keynote addresses. All I can say is, 'Y'all are doggone good coaches.'"

What they expressed didn't have a semblance of humor appreciation in it. Some folks just don't see any humor in anything, do they?

The basketball team was behind 58-14 at the half, and the coach was furious. As he tried to fire up his team in the locker room, he said, "I'm going over the basics of basketball with you one more time! Now listen to me!"

He picked up a basketball and said to the team, "This thing in my hands is a basketball! It is a regulation-size basketball! It holds nine pounds of air!"

Before he could continue, his star forward said, "Hey, coach, don't take it so fast."

Not funny to the coach.

I am fairly familiar with the notions of rural people. Rural people are great, but they sometimes have ideas about religion that are, well, different.

There are a few people in some rural areas in the South who believe that preachers ought not to receive any formal education. They believe that God will tell the preachers what to say and how to say it. I have talked to some who think that preachers have been "messed up" by going to college or seminary. I am not making fun of people's ideas, mind you, just relating them.

In a rural church there was a prominent member who passionately believed that preachers should not be formally educated. The pastor didn't share that opinion, so he invited a highly-educated minister out to the church to preach one of the services, for he thought the church would benefit from hearing such a learned man.

During the service, the pastor wanted to involve the member who disdained educated ministers, so he asked him to lead in the morning prayer. The only way the man could think of to show how much he resented the educated preacher's knowledge was to express his feelings in his prayer. So he prayed; "Oh, Lord, I thank Thee that Thou hast made me ignorant, and I pray that Thou wouldest make me ignoranter and ignoranter and ignoranter."

When the visiting preacher began speaking to the congregation, he said, "You know, that prayer the brother prayed awhile ago is the only one I've ever heard that was answered before it was asked."

Needless to say, the fellow who offered the prayer failed to see any humor in the preacher's observation.

Were you ever in the company of people who had no sense of humor? Me too. Aren't they fun? Lord, have mercy. Their skin is a little thin. Look there on their sleeves. Their feelings are showing. No humor. What a pity!

Wouldn't it be great if everyone got the message? Some things really don't *matter*. Everything isn't a big deal. All dark clouds don't bring storms. It really is worthwhile to laugh, especially at yourself.

If something bad in life pops it to you, a healthy sense of humor can remove the sting. If your disposition starts heating up, a healthy sense of humor can cool you off. Humor helps to soften the bumps in life's road. It helps to relieve the stress that has its grip on your emotional winding stem. It is restful and relaxing. It's a magnificent diversion. Nothing can help you put things into perspective like a healthy sense of humor.

If you will train yourself to see and to appreciate the humorous, your life will be more vibrant and radiant, and you'll be a heap happier.

Humor has value that transcends itself. It is not an end in itself, but it's a mighty good means to one. It's not a way out of life, but a way into it. The very least it can do for you is to make your life more livable. Anything that can do that is worth something, don't you think?

It is refreshing to meet folks who have learned the value of a healthy sense of humor. They are a tonic for the soul. It does me good to meet or to hear about folks who are actually *enjoying* life, and a sense of humor is a positive indicator of such enjoyment.

My brother-in-law, Dean Strickland, told me about one of his visits to his doctor. The doctor was preparing to do an examination requiring the use of latex gloves and K-Y Jelly. Dean asked the doctor to use two fingers. The doctor said, "Why?"

Dean said, "I want at least two opinions."

The doctor, appreciating the humor, said, "I'll use my entire hand, and we'll have a conference."

There is something special about folks who have a healthy sense of humor. They even make the air around them more fun to breathe.

I was on a plane seated beside an attractive, senior adult lady. We struck up a conversation. She was a retired teacher headed home to Florida. We talked about her community and her career and her trip. I asked her about her family. She had never been married, she told me. I asked, "How did a beautiful, sweet lady like you escape getting married?"

Her eyes twinkled as she replied, "I've always thought that men were like dresses."

"Like dresses?" I asked.

She smiled really big and said, "Yeah, there's always a better one on the next rack."

That lady won my heart right off the bat with her keen, delicious sense of humor. It's fun to be around people like her.

The preacher said, "If there is anyone in this congregation who does not have any enemies, please stand."

A little man of many years struggled to his feet.

The preacher said, "Brother, why don't you have any enemies?"

With a grin, the little man replied, "Outlived 'em."

There is nothing else in the world like a good, healthy sense of humor.

After a meeting at which I had spoken in Fredericksburg, Virginia, a farmer gentleman walked over to me and said, "When I die, I want a closed-casket funeral."

His comment drew me up short, leaving me not knowing how to respond or if I should respond, but he was smiling, and he just stood there looking at me, so I assumed he wanted me to say something.

Not being able to think of anything else to say, I asked, "Why's that?"

He said, "I want everybody I know to wonder if I'm *really* in there."

His delightful sense of humor made that evening for me. He was itching all over to see if he could get me to laugh. He could and I did.

A friend said to me the other day, "I wish today was Friday."

Kiddingly I said, "You wanna wish your life away?"

He thought a minute, then he said, "Well, I wish it was *last* Friday."

He gets points for his sense of humor; he also gets bonus points for being able to think fast.

An elderly gentleman I had just met caught my attention. He stood tall and erect; impeccably dressed, his appearance exuded dignity. After we had been introduced, he immediately said, "Guess how old I am."

I guessed, "About seventy?"

He said, "Nope. I'm ninety-two."

"Hope I look as good as you do when I'm ninety-two," I said.

With a wide smile, he said, "You don't look this good *now*."

What a great thing a healthy sense of humor is!

In my adult life, calling upon my sense of humor to bail me out of situations that otherwise would have ruffled my feathers has always been an enormous help to me. Testing has come to me often, but so far my sense of humor has remained intact, and it has bailed me out more times than I can remember. One of my most important discoveries in life is that a healthy sense of humor is too effective not to use, and it is too precious to lose.

Using as many humorous stories as I could think of to punctuate the points in my speech, I thought everything had gone pretty well. I did, at least, until a lady asked me afterward, "Do you mind if I tell you a *real* joke?"

Test! Test! Test!

A friendly airline agent once asked me, "Where do want to sit, aisle or window?"

Before I could respond, the captain of my flight said, "Put him by a window. That way, if we go down, he can see where we're headed."

Knowing that I was flying with a pilot who had a sense of humor made me feel so much better. Some airline captains I have met are aloof and unapproachable. This one wasn't. I appreciate him.

After one of my excellent speeches, a lady asked me, "Do you ever give talks that are humorous?"

The tests go on and on.

When I was teaching in a high school, during recess one day, a group of students came up to me in the hall. One of the girls in the group asked, "Mr. Ates, do you know what a really satisfied woman says?"

"I don't believe I do," was my reply.

She said, "I didn't think you would."

She and her friends laughed hysterically as they walked away. I thought it was funny, too. Incidentally, they never did let me forget that thing.

They tested my sense of humor. I made a pretty good grade, but the test wasn't easy.

Matching clothes has never been easy for me. Coordinating colors and patterns is not my thing.

One evening, heading out to speak at a meeting at a country club, and knowing that my appearance would be particularly important, I went by a clothing store to ask a professional if my clothes were appropriate. Going into the store, I asked a salesperson, "Does this tie go?"

He said, "Yes, it goes with something."

The tests come from every which way, but failure hasn't caught up with me yet. My sense of humor always has come to my rescue.

When I was in the pastorate, one of the church members asked me, "Do you have to spend a lot of time repairing your sermons?"

"Repairing?"

I thought, *Surely he meant "preparing."*

I could have emitted some sarcastic comment, but I didn't. I laughed. Now that I think about what he said from a more objective viewpoint, the sermons would have been much better if they had had more "preparing" and "repairing."

The officer who stopped me on an interstate asked politely, "What's your hurry, sir?"

"My meeting begins in fifteen minutes. I'm doing my best not to be late."

The courteous officer said, "Since you are in a big hurry, I'll write your ticket as fast as I can." He almost caused me to flunk my sense of humor test. It wouldn't have helped me if I had, though, so I said to myself, *Laugh, Wayne, you're already late.*

There were halls, rooms, and offices sprawled out all over the place in the rather large officers club building where the officers' wives were meeting. After asking for help, I finally found the meeting room.

Assuming that some of the wives were Yankees, and being a faithful southerner, I picked on the Yankees present in my inimitable, good-natured way. No one was offended, mind you. It was just good-hearted fun.

After the meeting, as I was trying to find my way out of the building and winding up on the side of it opposite the exit I needed, I finally asked for help.

One of the Yankee ladies turned toward me and said, "If you were a Yankee, you would have a better sense of direction."

There was nothing else for me to do except to laugh with her and all the others nearby who had heard what she had said. A sense of humor has such comforting power.

Oh, by the way, on this healthy sense of humor subject, it's vitally important to remember this: if you can't catch it, don't throw it.

All of us are tested occasionally. It's wise not to take ourselves overly seriously. There are some things we must take seriously, but let's be careful about taking ourselves overly seriously. Making that distinction is vital. Not to do so can result in all kinds of problems for you and for others around you.

All of us are extremely important. We all have dignity and worth, and no reasonable person would dispute that. To have a healthy sense of humor doesn't mean that one has to surrender any sense of dignity or worth. It does mean that we should not be so serious and sensitive about ourselves that we lose the ability to laugh.

Learning to laugh at ourselves and at many of the things that happen to us is the icing on life's cake. For our own sake, if for no other reason, we'd better learn the value of a healthy sense of humor. We can't be good livers without it.

Life is Communicating

During dinner, a guest said, "Such as it is, this food is very good."

He then thought, *That didn't sound right. Better rephrase it.*

Then he said, "For what little bit there is of it, this food is very good."

No better off, was he?

There is a vast difference between having something to say and knowing how to say it and feeling a need to say something, but doing it in a way that clearly shows that the obligation should not have been taken on.

Communicating well is a real chore. There are many things we do in life that are difficult, but one of the toughest tasks is to communicate effectively and clearly. Not many folks can do it. The problem is not that we lack the means and technology with which to get the communication job done well. After all, this is the information age; nonetheless, we often misunderstand and are often misunderstood.

A senior adult gentleman went to a physician and said, "Doc, I want something to kill my wife with. I'm tired of her, and I want to get rid of her."

The doc replied, "You know I can't do that. Tell you what, though, you can love her to death in three weeks. I mean really pour it on for three weeks, and it'll kill her as dead as a wedge."

The man brightened up and asked, "Will it really?"

The doc answered, "Yes, siree, it really will."

After two weeks had passed, the doctor thought, *I was just kidding that fellow about killing his wife. I'd better go over and check on him.*

In his Mercedes, the doctor drove up to the couple's house. Going inside, he saw the elderly husband in the den on a lounge chair. In spite of a roaring fire in the fireplace, the fellow was buried beneath four heavy quilts. His eyes were sunken, his complexion was pale and he was trembling as if he were having a chill. His wife was in the kitchen singing happily as she cooked dinner.

After observing the situation, the doc said, "Well, John, it looks pretty bad, doesn't it?"

"Yeah, it does, doc," the man said with a raspy, quivering voice. "She's back there just as happy as a lark, and I ain't got the heart to tell her she ain't gonna live but a week."

Sometimes it's easy to misunderstand, isn't it?

A college professor told me about a paper that one of his students submitted. He said that the student had written an engaging narrative about the town he was from, concluding the paper with, "If you ever get a chance to visit the town I'm from, I hope you'll take it." The professor said, "I don't know if the student meant for me to take the *chance* or to take the *town*."

I admire the student's pride in his home town, but his communication is a bit lacking, isn't it?

No matter who attempts it, communicating effectively is an enormous and an exacting problem for all of us.

While watching TV the other night, I got to wondering why the commercials are so effective. I suppose it's because they communicate so well. How do they do it? What accounts for the effectiveness of commercials?

They get the job done well because they are simple, concise, pointed, focused, brief, and repetitive. It's hard to miss the points, for the ads get to them and stay with them. Indeed, the points *in* the commercials are the points *of* the commercials. They don't dilly-dally about saying what they want to say. They send their messages and get out of there quickly. They omit extraneous, fluff material. In good ads, only the essentials are essential, and they come at us repeatedly until some of us memorize those essentials. The ads get attention and they deliver their messages, and they do both extremely well.

It's not that easy for everybody. When it comes to the science and art of communication, a lot of people don't know much, and I don't know much either. Communicating well is difficult for me, and just about everybody else is in the same boat. It's a difficult thing to do well.

Miscommunication, poor communication, and no communication are problems everywhere. In everyday conversations, in homes, in schools, in businesses, in governments, in industries, and in places of worship, breakdowns in communication occur all the time. It's tough to get it right, yet we have to keep trying, because it's too important not to.

We all have to spend much effort trying to communicate in a myriad of circumstances. The whole fabric of life is woven with communication. It's the way we operate. Life *is* communicating. Information and people are continuously being brought together. We can't function any other way.

Folks say some interesting and sometimes humorous things as they attempt to communicate. Once in a rare while even I say things that don't make sense. Do you ever do that?

A lady was commenting to her husband about how fortunate they had been in having such well-behaved children. She talked about how they had had no really serious problems with their children in terms of drinking, drugs, sex, and other areas in which youngsters can cause their parents a lot of grief. She continued, "Many teenagers these days are getting married out of wedlock."

Her husband asked, "What did you say?"

She repeated the comment about teenagers getting married out of wedlock. It still didn't register with her what she had said until her husband repeated it to her. She then said, "Aw, you know what I meant. I meant having children out of wedlock, not getting married out of wedlock."

Sometimes the idea is there, but the words we say don't fit. Linking words to ideas is a challenging process. That's what communication is all about. Maybe that's why it's so hard to get it right.

During a trial, a lawyer asked a young lady who was a friend of the defendant, "What's your relationship to the accused?"

The witness smiled and responded, "Fine!"

Communication. What a problem!

I went to the college security office to pick up an identification decal for my vehicle.

After looking at my paperwork, a lady in there took my money for the fee, handed me the decal, and instructed me to; "Put this decal on the left rear bumper of your car."

I studied her instruction for a little bit, and then I asked, "What was that?"

She repeated with her voice raised a notch, "Put your decal on the left rear bumper of your car."

Sounds exactly like what she said before, I thought.

Her instruction made no sense to me. I said to her, "I have only one rear bumper on my car. I don't have a left rear bumper and a right rear bumper nor any other bumper in any other position on the rear of my car. I have one rear bumper. I don't understand what you mean about the 'left rear bumper.'"

She semi-yelled, "Put your decal on the left side of your rear bumper!"

Now the instruction made sense. Why didn't she say that to begin with?

Most of the time when we misunderstand someone or when someone misunderstands us, it is because we spoke or wrote unclearly. Most of us can understand communication that is too clear to be misunderstood. That's the way it ought to be all the time. At least we should aim for it. Communication is best when it's plain and simple.

All good communicators make their messages clear. They aim to help folks understand by doing all they can to prevent any misunderstanding.

Some fence builders were putting up a fence around my pasture. I joked with one of the workers by asking him, "How long does it take to build a fence?"

He gave me a look that said, *What kind of a stupid question is that?* Then he said, "Depends on what kind it is, how high it is, and how long it is."

My question was jokingly unclear, but his answer was clear as crystal. I had no problem knowing exactly what he meant.

Above all else, communication demands clarity, for without it, the loss in terms of effective communication is irreparable. Of course, for you to make something clear to others, it must be clear to you.

A family was at the dinner table all ready to enjoy the meal. Mother looked at her pre-school daughter and asked, "Would you ask the blessing for us?"

The little girl said, "No, ma'am."

The mother said, "And what will God think if you don't ask the blessing?"

Her daughter answered, "He will think we're not going to eat tonight."

It was clear to her, and it's as clear as a sun-drenched day to me.

A teacher asked a student, "Are you afraid of the dark?"

The student replied, "No, ma'am. Nobody in the dark can see me no better'n I can see him."

The grammar might need some work, but the communication is pricelessly clear. The student was clear in his thinking; consequently, he was clear in his communication. There is no way to misunderstand what he meant.

Tom Carter of Cordele, Georgia, told me that he and his wife, Charissa, were at a mall one day. They were trying to decide what to do, but nothing that either one suggested seemed to be what both of them wanted to do. Tom said that as he and his wife were talking, a man whom neither of them knew walked up and said, "Sir, the best thing for you to do is to find out what she wants to do and then make her do it."

Tom wisely said, "I don't know about the 'make' part, but what the man said was perfectly clear to me."

We studied a poem in one of the ninth grade classes I was teaching. Something about the concept of *time* came up in our discussion.

I said, "*Time* is a real poser for me. To have a good working definition of it would be very helpful."

One of my students said, "Mr. Ates, time is not an objective entity in the universe. It's a relative means by which we measure the passing of events. It's abstract, not concrete."

I sat there with my mouth open for a while, trying to make myself believe that this ninth grader had really said what I had just heard him say.

The words came out of his mouth like water from a fountain. What he was talking about was clear to him, and he made it clear to the rest of us, including the two students who arrived late. Of course, I first had to clear up for them the meanings of the words *objective, relative, entity, universe, concrete* and *abstract*.

Good communication is not fuzzy, ambiguous, or confusing. It is clear. If it leaves the gate open for a bunch of questions, something has gone wrong. Perspicuity is the *sine qua non* of effective communication.

A lady told me about an elderly man who consulted his doctor about a sweating problem he was experiencing.

He said, "Doc, I'm worried to death about myself. The first time my wife and I have a little session, I get along fine, but the second time I sweat, I sweat buckets, and I'm really worried."

The doctor did a thorough examination and said, "I don't find anything wrong with you. You are as fine as can be. I don't know what causes your sweating. Just one of those things. Don't worry about it. You're healthy."

A couple of weeks later, the gentleman's wife went to the same doctor. The subject about her husband's sweating problem came up.

Doc said, "I'm puzzled about that sweating. I don't have any idea what could cause it."

The lady said, "Oh, I know what causes it."

The physician was quite curious, so he asked, "What do you think it is?"

She answered, "It's a lot hotter in August than it is in January."

Clarity. What a precious thing. When you communicate clearly, folks don't have to spin their wheels trying to read your mind.

A student, talking to his English teacher, said, "I don't understand all this *Iliad* and *Odyssey* stuff."

The teacher replied, "But to pass this course, you must."

There is no substitute for clarity.

Some of the clearest and, therefore, the best communication I've ever heard has come from old-timers in various parts of our country. I don't know if the memorable things I've heard from them came from them originally or if they were repeating what someone else had said. It doesn't really matter. The important thing is that what I've heard them say is superb communication. The way some folks can put words together fascinates me.

Here are some of the most impressive lines that I recall from people who probably had no idea that anyone was interested in what they were saying, let alone that anyone would remember their words: "As straight as six o'clock;" "Lotta things coulda been done a long time ago if people had knowed how to do 'em;" "I don't need to know answers to questions I ain't never gonna be asked;" "The sharper the saw, the cleaner the cut;" "Any way you turn, you are still you;" "You can call it whatever you want to, but sin is still sin."

The folks who said those words wouldn't know the difference between a transitive verb and a perfect passive infinitive, but they could communicate truth with perfect clarity, and that's more important.

Fred was middle-aged when he developed diabetes. The disease caused foot sores which were reluctant to heal. One sore became so painful he could not tolerate a bed sheet touching it.

During a medical exam, Fred's doctor said, "Fred, you need to scrub that sore with a heavily soaped wash cloth. I mean scrub it hard."

Fred incredulously exclaimed, "Scrub it? Are you out of your mind? Scrubbing that thing would be like sandpapering my eyeball!"

Do you have any problem understanding what Fred was trying to communicate? I'll bet even the doctor understood it.

Fred didn't have to go into any more detail about how painful such a procedure would be. He went right to the heart of the matter with a sharply focused picture. However clear a bell is, that's how clear Fred was.

I was talking to a Louisiana state police officer about traffic situations that can cause accidents. I'll never forget one thing he said: "He who passes on hills and curves is not a man of iron nerves; he's crazy."

Statements like that are memorable. Why? Because they are clothed with clarity. Clear and memorable communication is high-quality stuff. Clear, definitive, and drawn-in-picture language works wonders every time.

Another essential component of good communication is brevity. One does not have to be inebriated with verbosity to communicate well. As a matter of fact, wordiness gets in the way of communication as few other obstacles can. Long-winded attempts at communication are an efficient way to bore the daylights out of people. I love it when speakers or writers get to the point quickly. There is a lot of merit in it. It is possible to be brief without being blunt. Most books and most speeches are too long.

A professor gave his students this excellent advice: "Your speeches should have a captivating introduction and a dynamic conclusion, and both of them should be close together."

Obviously, some subjects require more time or space to develop than others do, but the too long should be long gone. Enough is enough.

Effective communication cannot be achieved unless there is someone to intelligently receive it. A quarterback can throw excellent passes all year, but without an alert receiver, there is no hope of a touchdown. Communication works the same way.

Effective communication demands attention to what is being communicated, to whom it is directed, why it is being communicated, under what circumstances it is being communicated, when it is being communicated, how it is being communicated, who is communicating, and where it is being communicated. Communication is affected by the nature of the material, by the moods of the folks involved in the process, by tones of voices, by words or images, and by body language.

There are many communication factors that I don't know about, but I do know that attempting to communicate is something that we all do every day of our lives for this or that purpose; therefore, we need to do our best to be sure that we are not misunderstood.

For good livers, communicating well is not as easy as ABC, but it's just as basic.

Life is Believing

After a week of marriage, a husband said to his wife, "Now that we're married, I want to point out a few little defects I've noticed in you."

His wife said, "You go right ahead. It was them defects that kept me from gettin' a decent husband."

What a mess! That's the kind of thing that happens, though, when folks look for the "defects" in others or in themselves.

Self-destructive negativity is an affront to the intelligence and well-being of any rational human being, and it is a curse to all that is purposeful, meaningful, and fulfilling in life. It competes with everything that makes sense. It distorts; it twists; it vitiates. A negative mind is a junk closet. Negativity is a degenerative mental force at work which destroys the very best programs, plans, and projects.

I dislike negative, pessimistic thinking with every fiber of my being. Isn't it just great and encouraging to hear folks spout these kinds of rubbish?: "I can' t;" "It's impossible;" "It won't work;" "We never did it like that before;" "It ain't no good;" "Everything I do is wrong;" "I can't please anybody;" "The whole world stinks;" "It's too risky;" "Nobody likes me;" "I'm not appreciated;" "I'm afraid;" "There's no use to try;" "It's hopeless;" "I'm so depressed;" "I'm worried to death;" "I just don't know what I'm going to do;" "There's no way out of this mess;" "This problem is killing me;" "Nothing good ever happens to me;" "Nobody understands my situation;" "Just my luck." Inspiring, isn't it? Talk about springboards to progress. Lord, have mercy!

Lots of folks go through life believing and saying negative stuff like that all the time. No faith, no confidence, no positive expectations at all. They put the worst construction on the best of things. If there is a dark side to anything, they will doggone certainly find it. They'll hold on to their pessimism until their mental knuckles cramp.

A negative mind says, "I'll shoot to kill on sight any and all inspiring thoughts, any and all suggestions for improvement, any and all ideas implying inspiration, any and all hints of help, any and all routes to realization, any and all programs for progress, any and all ways to win, any and all noble notions, any and all appropriate answers, any and all menaces to mediocrity, any and all motivations to be more, any and all desires to develop, any and all wise words and any and all challenges to change. I'll turn them down; I'll turn them off; I'll turn them away." To people who think like that, the highways to the highest are closed.

It's pretty common to detect this pitiful kind of faithlessness and resignation anywhere you go. Intelligent optimism is running rather short these days.

Too many people work hard at perfecting their abilities to whine and pine, to groan and moan, and to grumble and complain. Every now and then I hear someone say, "I would have a more positive attitude, but . . ." "I would be more positive about situations and people, but . . ." But? But what?

The speaker was using notes while he addressed a group. When he came to a statement in his speech which contained the words, "Yes, but," his notes fell to the floor without his noticing. He said, "Yes, but," and he couldn't remember what came next. He didn't know where his notes had gotten off to. He stammered around saying, "Yes, but, uh, yes, but." He repeated, "Yes, but," several times and still couldn't collect his thoughts.

Someone in the audience said, "Your 'yes, but' is on the floor."

The floor is a good place for the *yes, but's* of life. A grave is an even better place for them.

I'm not going to waste valuable time and energy butting my head against the *yes, but's* of life. How about you? If we get stuck in the mud of the *yes, but's*, we'll accomplish only a lot of wheel spinning. One plain *yes* is better than *all* the *yes, but's*. Yes, to the things that are good, honorable, decent, worthy, and uplifting. Yes! Yes! What a tantalizing idea!

I wonder how negative thinking is supposed to help anybody. How is it supposed to make one's life better? How does it make progress possible? How is it useful? What's the point of it? What's the ultimate outcome of it? I wonder.

It is always appropriate to be negative about negativity. Sometimes it is certainly all right to be negative. *No* is a very useful word. But it's always terrible to be a negative thinker. What's the difference? Well, what's the difference between *sentiment* and *sentimentality*? The former is good. The latter is sickening. What's the difference between *argument* and *argumentative*? The former is fine when it's under control. The latter is disgusting.

Negativity is a destructive attitude. It adversely affects you and those around you. It gets you nowhere. It's the springboard of failure. It's the delivery room of worry. It's the seed of fear, the companion of stress, the partner of anxiety, and the bud of hopelessness. It will put your life in disarray in a hurry.

It is easier to keep away from negativity than it is to get away from it. You can't succeed if you're gripped with it. You might as well try to trim your toenails with an axe. A negative attitude ensures failure.

Can you imagine a teacher saying, "My students will never learn what I am trying to teach them?"

What would you think of a doctor who told you, "This medication I'm prescribing won't help you one bit?" How about a lawyer who said to you, "I'll take your case, but there's no way to win it?" What would be your opinion of a salesperson who thought, *I can't sell this merchandise?* What kind of outcome could be expected from a detective who believed, *I can't solve this crime?* What if the politician running for office said, "I'll never get elected?"

Those kinds of attitudes are unimaginable to me. It's hard to do what one doubts.

Anybody who ever did anything worth doing had to believe that it could be done. Otherwise, why would one even try? It would be out of the question for us to attempt anything unless we had hope that we could succeed. It just won't work for us to be opposed to our own success. Failure cannot be our preference. Failure to believe breeds failure to try, and failure to try is failure.

One of the few physicians I have ever known who was completely honest with me was not only a high quality medical professional, he was also my friend. One day while we were discussing my minor medical problem, I said, "You know, doc, I trust you absolutely."

He said, "Good. That's half the battle."

He was right, of course.

Sometimes trust is not just half the battle; it's the whole thing. If you can get to the believing point, the road to victory is not nearly so tough.

Ah, the battle. There is *always* the battle.

We can't afford to sit still and leave those discouraging, negative thoughts unchallenged. We have to take them on. When they attack, we have to fight back. I mean fight hard. No giving in to them. There must be no room in our minds for gloom or doom. Yeah, it's a battle. Perhaps *the* battle.

You cannot coexist with negativity any more than you can coexist with a malignancy. Stop it, or it will stop you. Negativity has the same death-dealing potential for your mind and spirit as the tumor does for your body. Being your own adversary is enough to whip you. There is no clout in doubt.

Negativity fails. It fails theoretically and practically. Without fail, it fails every time it's tried. If an approach fails every time it's tried, why insist on doing it that way? If you subtract faith and add doubt and multiply fear, you will divide yourself into hopelessly chaotic bits of failure. Negativity is not intelligent endeavoring. It is mental blindness.

The other day I asked a fellow, "What are you doing?"

He answered, "Nothing."

I said, "Kinda hard to tell when you get through, isn't it?"

To do *nothing* makes no sense to me. How can you do *nothing*? *Nothing* is a real poser for me. It's sort of slippery, hard to pin down. Have you ever tried to do *nothing*, to think of *nothing*?

The word *nothing* is like the word *impossible*. Negative thinkers thrive on both of those words. This line of thought is going somewhere, I promise. Hang on a jiffy.

Nothing is like *impossible* because neither one of them can be. There is no such thing as *nothing*. There is no such thing as *impossible*. Well, do you know what they are? I don't either.

Nothing is not and cannot be, and the impossible has never happened, and it won't.

I have read a bunch of books in which authors wrote about how all of us should attempt the impossible, believe in the impossible, reach for the impossible. There are even songs with those kinds of ideas in them. All of that stuff about the impossible and what we ought to do with it sounds good for a writer, speaker, or lyricist to use, but what sense does it make? That's my problem. I'll try to show you what I mean.

The impossible is, by definition, "not possible." The possible is possible, but the impossible isn't. Sometimes what folks think is impossible is possible, but they render it impossible by failing to believe that it is possible. There is a vast difference between what is actually impossible and what people *believe* to be impossible.

It's out of rational bounds to *believe* that the impossible is possible. It's also out of rational bounds to surrender to the notion that the possible is impossible.

There is a great gulf fixed between what seems to be and what really is. A goal might seem to be impossible when it really isn't. It's limited only in the mind, but that, sad to say, is limitation enough.

If you believe that the possible is impossible, you are whipped from the start. You won't lift up; you'll fold up. But if you believe that the possible is possible, you have the appropriate attitude crucial to creative action. You will get after it because you believe that what can be *can be*. You won't pursue goals because you believe that what cannot be can be. That wouldn't make any sense at all, and to be sure, there is nothing irrational about a believing attitude. It makes good sense to believe in the possibility of the possible. Extremely good sense.

I don't know what is possible and what isn't. I do know that only the possible is possible. Sometimes the predictable must be defied so that the possible can be detected.

Did any of my goings on about *nothing* and *impossible* and *possible* make any sense to you? It was about sense, but did it *make* sense? What I have written might seen to be as awkward as a pig on roller skates, but I really do believe that attitude is precisely where the battle is waged. If one's attitude is bad, everything else is too. If one's attitude is good, everything else follows as a matter of course.

A positive attitude is vital in life, but some practical, common sense actions are needed to complement it. Faith puts bait on the hook. "Faith without works is dead," as the Good Book puts it.

"Truer words were never spoken," is the way my mama would say it.

Faith can be dead? You bet it can. The thing that's important about faith is not whether you have a little or a lot of it, not whether it's weak or strong, but whether it's alive. Faith that's alive is faith that's active.

It is that positive, active approach that creates energy, purpose, and success. Attitude affects actions. Belief determines behavior. A positive attitude is not the tool of a fool. It is the foundation of all realistic effort.

Good attitude and good action have *big* written all over them. We need to think bigger, act bigger, and, consequently, be bigger. Kids talk about what they are going to be when they get *big*. What do you want to be when your attitude and your actions get *big*?

We need to think of ways to do things rather than concentrating on why we can't do them. Let's ask, "What's right with it? What's good about it?"

Really and truly, in spite of all the pervasive negative approaches to life and in spite of all the lugubrious prognostications that come along, there is more good around than there is bad. There is more right than there is wrong. There is more cause for hope than for despair. There is more success than there is failure. There is more cause for rejoicing than for rejecting. There is more togetherness than there is division. There is more to celebrate than there is to criticize. Wouldn't all of us be better off if we would really concentrate on the positive aspects of life? Couldn't we just try it and see how it works out? Whatever anyone else does, you and I can try it, can't we?

Someone was complaining to me the other day about his struggle with bad circumstances. I said, "Well, think of all the bad you have *missed* in your life."

That seemed to help his attitude somewhat.

He smiled slightly and said, "Yeah, you're right. This little thang ain't goin' to amount to nothin' nohow."

He was exactly right. The good things in your life will just about overwhelm you if you seriously think about them for a while. Why don't you try doing that? The resulting difference in your attitude will make a real difference in your life.

Not only do we need a positive attitude about ourselves, we need to think positively about other folks. There is a whole lot of *puttin' folks down* going on. It's so easy to participate in fault-finding criticism of other people. It's so easy to get caught up in the gossip trap. Some people take pleasure in making others look bad. That's a crying shame.

Say about people only what you would be willing to put your signature to. That practice would help you to make yourself quit putting up with putting people down.

There is no way to help other people if we don't believe in them, and helping folks is what makes the wheels go round, you know. Gotta believe in 'em.

I've made many mistakes in my life. No matter what you have heard about me, I am not perfect. Failing to believe in people and failing to expect the best from them are not mistakes, however, that I intend to make.

When I was teaching in high school, I had a student who had not been doing extraordinarily high quality work in my class. It was lousy, to tell the truth. He and I had a little chat about it. He said he believed he could do better and that he would try. I believed him and, more importantly, I believed *in* him.

Not long after the conference, I gave a test. The student made a score of 96. I was ecstatic. At recess, I took his test paper to the principal. When I showed him the good report he said, "Ates, that student is not capable of doing work like that." My reply to him is one reason I am not teaching now.

I left him and went to the guidance counselor. She glanced at the paper I showed her, she pulled out a file on the student and said, "According to his test scores, he's unable to perform on that level."

Both the principal and the guidance counselor believed the student could not possibly do the work that he obviously had done. Somebody, please help me figure all this out. How can he not be able to do it? I have demonstrable proof that he can do it. The fact is irrefutable.

The student believed in himself. He had a teacher who believed in him, too. I gave him the work, he accepted the work and he did a good job with it. He kept on doing it, mind you.

It is amazing what folks will do if they know that somebody believes in them. "You can lead a horse to water, but you can't make him drink," I'm told. Maybe so, but he'll drink if you give him some salt first.

It's important to be positive about ourselves. It's important to be positive about other folks. Additionally, we should be positive about the future.

A corporate president said, "It's easy to predict the future. It's the present we can't seem to sort out."

Well, I guess we all hope the future will be there when we get there. One thing is for certain, there's no point in worrying about it.

I'm not an expert in anything, let alone the future, but I do believe that a whole lot of people are spending a bunch of valuable time and effort worrying about tomorrow. Seems to be a big item nowadays. Parents worry. Kids worry. Business people worry. Professionals worry. Farmers worry. Workers worry. Lenders worry. Borrowers worry. Poor folks worry. Rich folks worry. Worry must be about as widespread as the common cold. It seems to fit right in with modern, high-speed, stress-filled life. I guess we're all expected to do it. Seems trendy enough.

Well, I reckon you expect me to take a different view. Glad to oblige.

Worry is one of the most foolish exercises in futility on earth. We all need a little tension to make us tick, but worry will wind us up so tight our tickers might snap. Worry is tension taken to excess, and none of us needs that.

Worry is a deliberate choice to erect an imaginary obstacle that incarcerates us within the confines of a foolish failure that would not and could not occur otherwise.

Worry takes too much time, effort, and imagination. Can't comment about you, but I can't afford the time; I'm too lazy to expend the effort; I'm not fertile enough in my imagination. It looks like I'll have to be counted out of the worry business, for I don't have what it takes to participate.

Worry has never helped me. Oh, yes, I've tried it. I used to do it a lot until I found out that the only way I could be a good liver was to live one event at a time and not to worry about the next one. I've been doing that for several years now. Seems to work pretty well.

Another thing I've noticed about worry is that it tends to be self-centered. Worriers concentrate on themselves too much. They are their main attraction. It wouldn't be such a big deal otherwise, would it? Don't you see? Worry is self-centered and a self-centered life is pathetic.

There are all kinds of problems associated with worry. It can have deeply serious ramifications.

On the other hand, there's faith; there's confidence; there's that refreshing positive attitude. The main thing that I like about faith is that it frees me from worry and anxiety about the future so that I can live a creative, purposeful, and happy life in the present. Faith gives me a liberating independence from external circumstances which would crush me if I tried to live life with a cold, negative attitude. I believe that faith, the positive approach, is the key to authentic existence. It does not make the way easy, but it does make it possible. That's enough to make the journey exciting.

Whatever the future holds for us, let us not let worry strangle our hopes and dreams. Let us not allow worry to cloud our vision. Let us not let worry affect our tomorrows.

Nothing in our lives is more devastating than a negative attitude no matter what form it takes and no matter how it is directed. It destroys everything it touches. It has no redeeming value whatsoever.

John married a lady named Lillie. They were together for several years. Lillie died. A couple of years later John married a woman named Tillie. They were together for several years. Tillie died and was buried in the same plot as Lillie with enough room between the two for John's grave. John later told some of his friends, "When I die, be sure to bury me between Lillie and Tillie, but please tilt me just a little toward Lillie."

Negative thinker, how about tilting your thinking just a little toward the positive. Tilt it over that way. Try it. The more you try it, the more you'll like it. Tilt your thinking toward the bright side. There's more light over there. You'll be better able to see over there where the light's shining.

The preacher had preached about two hours. After that, he spent another hour asking for people to come on to the front and join the church. Finally a young fellow went up to the front, thinking to himself, *I'm about to starve. I'm gonna join, so I can go home and eat.*

The preacher was so excited that he had a *candidate for baptism* that he asked two of the deacons to escort the young man to his home so he could prepare himself for baptism. The preacher told the deacons, "You make sure to bring him to the river. Don't let him get away from you."

Well, the young fellow and the deacons went to the baptismal candidate's house. As the young man came through the kitchen on his way out to where the deacons were waiting, he noticed on the dining table some biscuits left over from breakfast. He quickly ate one of the biscuits and stuffed two more of them into his overall pocket. The two deacons watched him so closely he felt a little self-conscious about attempting to eat the other two biscuits, so he left them in his pocket.

At the river, as the preacher lowered the young man into the water, the uneaten biscuits became waterlogged and floated to the surface of the water. A lady on the river bank shouted out, "Put him under again, preacher, the sin is coming out of him in chunks."

That's the way negative attitudes should come out of folks, in chunks. Let 'em go! They have hobbled, chained, and shackled you long enough! Enough is enough! The tragedy is not that life is brief but that for so long so many postpone its starting time.

The most important thing about you is your attitude, and the most important thing about your attitude is that it be positive. Life can unfold for you if you believe. Your journey will assume such a quality and depth that you will wonder why you waited so long to get on with it.

The good livers don't go through life wondering; they go through it wonderfully.

Life is Determination-ing

A roadside cafe with a large front porch sat next to a highway out in the country. At one end of the porch were seated two elderly ladies who were passing a little time together after they had eaten lunch. At the other end of the porch was a truck driver who was resting up before he hit the road.

A tractor pulling a trailer heavily loaded with shelled corn passed by in front of the cafe. Some of the kernels dribbled off the sides of the trailer onto the road and along the shoulder.

Soon after the tractor passed by, an old hen ran from the side of the cafe with a rooster chasing right behind her. If you know country life, you've see that same kind of thing happen often enough.

The hen ran smack out onto the road, and a car hit her, killing her instantly.

The rooster spotted the corn on the shoulder of the road, stopped, and began eating his fill, oblivious to the fate of the hen.

One of the ladies on the porch said to the other, "Would you look at that? That hen gave her life for her principles."

The truck driver, having also witnessed the chicken-rooster episode, muttered to himself, "I hope I never get that hungry."

Points of view, huh?

Determination is hunger. Good livers are hungry people, hungry in terms of their desires to be more, to be better, to be excellent. They are not satisfied with business as usual. They are not couched within the confines of the devices of a ho-hum satisfaction. They are persistent and insistent and consistent when it comes to their desires to be excellent, and they are resistant to obstacles and discouragement which threaten worthy performance. In short, they have determination. They have grit; therefore, they will not quit. Momentum has a way of rewarding those who refuse to quit. Life in its fullness is like education or happiness. It's not for everybody, just for those who hunger for it.

Have you ever known folks who were determined? They refused to fail on purpose? They didn't have any give up plays in their game plans? Their *intents* determined their *extents*?

From people who are determined, you won't hear resigned comments like: "I can't go on;" "I'm washed up;" "I've had it;" "It's hopeless;" "I don't care any more." No, no. Folks who are determined are gripped by a passion to go on. They won't lose interest. They won't be languid. They won't be listless. They won't be devitalized. We need more of that brand of folks.

A child saw some lightning bugs. He asked his grandpa, "What makes lightning bugs light up?"

Grandpa didn't know, so he did what any decent grandpa in that situation would do. He said, "I'll tell you tomorrow."

The little guy wasn't satisfied with that evasion. He decided to catch one of the bugs and see for himself what made them light up. As he caught one of the bugs, he inadvertently mashed it in his hand. He ran over to his grandpa and exclaimed excitedly, "Grandpa, I found out what makes 'em light up. The stuff's on the inside!"

Oh, yeah, that's where determination is. It's the inside stuff that makes you light up, making you what you are and keeping you from being what you are not. It makes you go on.

I have seen determination do things that nothing else could do, overcoming apparently insurmountable obstacles, accomplishing virtual miracles. You have seen it too, haven't you?

At a church in the country, a committee meeting was in progress. One of the members became angry because of something the pastor said.

He threatened the preacher by yelling. "If you don't shut up, I'll throw you through that window!"

The preacher smiled and replied, "Well, brother, maybe you will throw me through that window, but when you get home and your wife sees your bloody face, and when you explain to her how you got it, she'll say, 'The preacher didn't want you to throw him through that window, did he?'"

Winning presupposes wanting. Determination is a good driver, and aspiration is a good animator.

Don't give up. You might be only one decision away from life as you really can live it. Go on. Toughen up. Go on. When you can't see any way out, go on. When problems pound you, go on. When everything you touch tumbles and crumbles, go on. Go on when it's the toughest thing for you to do. Go on. Go on.

It's not always easy to go on, but determination says, "There is only one way for me to go, and that is forward." Life is often a crunch instead of a cruise. Determination doesn't spell facility; it spells adversity, and, if you look for them, you'll find a lot of advantages in adversity. There are no bargains on the counter. There is no cheap way to make the climb. Challenges will present themselves. Go on. Foes will line up against you. Go on. Circumstances will threaten you and fears will engulf you. Go on. Life is not always tidy; sometimes it's tough. Go on. It's not always fun; sometimes it's frustrating. Go on. When you are tired, keep on trying. Go on. Go on.

A boxer stepped into a ring. He gave two upper cuts, a straight left, and a few jabs. Then the fellow he was supposed to box got into the ring.

It's easy to go on when nothing is in your way, but when something keeps popping you in the face, it takes something extra. That *something extra* is determination, and we all need a big supply of it.

When adversity threatens to press you down and tries to make you lose your nerve, remember, you were made for difficult times. If life were easy, it would be unbearably boring. If life were easy, everyone would get it right, but everyone doesn't because it isn't. The best means battle. Triumph means trial. Determination will not remove life's obstacles, but it will give you the heart to hurdle them. Whatever happens, don't quit the fight. Determination is not a lullaby to lull you to sleep. It is a bugle blast that calls you onward, forward, and upward. Go on. You must not stop. You dare not stop. You cannot stop. Go on. Go on.

You'll make mistakes, sometimes even a mess. You might be inclined to cry over spilled milk. What should you do instead? Clean up the mess, learn what you can from it; then go on. Go on.

My question to Dr. Kenneth Ross of Rome, Georgia, was, "What's the first thing that pops into your mind when I say the word *determination?*"

He immediately responded, "Love."

I said, "Love?"

He said, "Yeah, love is both the motivation for and the reward for determination."

He lost me at first, but it became clearer to me as he elaborated. He said that if you love what you do, if you love your family and yourself, if you love other folks, you will be determined to succeed for yourself and for the others whom you love.

I had never thought about it that way before. Determination is not only hunger, it is also love.

There has to be something more to determination than just stickability, more than just completing the task. That something more is love. Determination emanates from a love that is so intense it needs no supplementation. I wish I had thought of all that. My friend, you threw a whole new light on the thing for me, and I thank you.

Determination is hunger; it is love and it is one's willingness to sacrifice in order to reach a goal. An old man suffers aches and pains in order to grow a garden. The joy of one outweighs the agony of the other.

Determination manifests itself in purposeful action. You can't sit on the sideline and watch while others play the game. Determination doesn't sit around watching. It gets into the game. Determined people are compelled and propelled. Determination breeds urgent, intelligent action.

I was involved in a major automobile accident several years ago. My eyes were severely damaged, being covered for a week or so while I was in the hospital.

Calling for help one day so that I could get to and from the restroom, I asked an orderly if it would be all right for me to get out of bed to go.

He said, "Yes, Sir, you can go to the restroom if you've got the urgency."

I thought to myself, *Do I ever have the urgency?* I didn't say so to him, but I had the urge, too.

Determination gives you a sense of urgency. You don't hesitate and argue if you're determined. You don't postpone the important stuff. To do nothing is the worst error. You have to go on. You have to get rid of the "will not" power. Remember, all greatness is marked by determination.

Determination spells the difference between the satisfaction of a life well-lived and the shabby satisfaction of not caring how it is lived. The good livers are always aware of that vital distinction.

Life is Aiming

There is nothing like the confidence born of knowing what you want to accomplish and why. If you don't know where you want to go, there is no telling where you will wind up, and there is no telling what condition you will be in when you get there.

I enjoy unique expressions whether written or spoken. A friend of mine who spent some time in north Georgia said that some north Georgia folks use the expression, "There ain't no knowing." I gathered from what he said about it that it means something like, *There is no real answer,* or *It's a puzzle to me,* or *It's impossible to know the meaning,* or *No one can understand the situation.* I think my loose translation is fairly close to the original intended meaning.

If one tries to live a successful life on a personal and/or professional level without worthy objectives, *there ain't no knowing* where that person is headed. As we say in south Georgia, "there ain't no telling" what the outcome of such an endeavor would be. I believe *there ain't no knowing* must precede *there ain't no telling* because if you don't know, you surely can't tell.

Often I ask myself, *Are my efforts worth my life? What difference is my life going to make to anyone besides me? Are my goals really worthy? Are my efforts doing anybody any good?*

Those questions are serious. Asking them of myself to make doubly sure that I stay on track is extremely helpful to me. Please take the time to ask the same or similar questions of yourself. While you're at it, it wouldn't be a bad idea to review the answers too. Try to be as objective as you can about your objectives.

A man and his wife were having a great time at a carnival. They had spent all their money except a dime, and the man insisted on spending it on a merry-go-round ride for himself. His wife said, "No, now, don't ride that thing. Let's keep the dime and spend it on something worthwhile."

The husband insisted, "I ain't never rode one of them things, and I'm gonna ride it."

And so he did.

When he got off and walked over to his wife, she said to him, "O.K., look at what you did. You rode it. You spent our last dime, you went round and round, you got off where you got on, and you ain't been nowhere."

That is precisely what happens when one has no clearly defined goals in life. You go round and round, but you really go nowhere.

A woman lay dying. Her doctor told her that her remaining time on earth was very brief. She said, "I can't die yet. I haven't figured out why I've been living."

Have you figured it out for yourself yet?

I'm not trying to be profoundly philosophical here, delving into the nature of our being, probing into the nature of human existence and all that kind of abstract stuff. I'll leave that sort of exercise to someone who is qualified to do it.

I'm talking about you and me and what we are doing with our lives. I'm talking concrete reality here. What are you doing that is worthwhile? To what end or purpose are you living? Those questions are really not that difficult. Either you know the answers or you don't.

There are some things in life that we need to be sure of, and one of those things concerns the direction, the purpose, the goal, the aim of our lives. If we suddenly reached our goals, where would we be? What would we be? What would we have? What difference would any of our attainments have made? Sobering questions.

Down here in the South, a lot of folks say, "Shore," when they mean *sure* or *surely* or *certainly* as in, *He shore did*, or *Shore 'nuff*.

I knew a fellow who asked me nearly every time I saw him, "Wayne, what do you know for shore? You've been to a lot of schools, so what do you really know for shore?"

I would just smile and say, "I don't know very much."

One day he caught me when I wasn't feeling very good. He said, "Hey, Wayne, what do you know for shore today?"

I said, "Brother, I know one thing for shore. A snake can't straddle a log."

He never asked me that question again. My answer must have satisfied him.

Incidentally, I realize that what I told him is not useful knowledge, but it was all that came to my mind at the moment. I wish I had thought of it before then; maybe he would have left me alone sooner.

By the way, how would you have answered him?

I wish I had more and better answers to ridiculous questions, because I get more than my fair share of them. Ridiculous questions, mind you, not ridiculous questioners.

Someone asked me the other day, "How long would it take for someone to dig half a hole?"

I said, "I don't have the foggiest idea."

He knew he had me. He said, "Nobody can dig half a hole because a hole of any size is a whole hole."

He thought I was really stupid not to know the correct answer.

Why questions like that find their way to me is beyond my comprehension.

There are some things that we need to be certain about, however. What are you aiming for? Come on, now, think about it. Be honest with yourself. Clear answer, or is it about as fuzzy as a politician's answer during an interview?

Haven't you known folks who didn't make it in life because their goals were not clear to them? They had just about everything that anyone could possibly want or need: time, intelligence, education, training, personality, ability, capability; all that good stuff. They even had desire, I warrant. Didn't they want success? They probably would have achieved it if they had just been able to figure out where they wanted to go. That kind of uncertainty has put lots of good folks in the fog.

The basketball players come out onto the court, getting ready to warm up prior to the game. They look all around the gymnasium, and, lo and behold, there are no goals in there. They bring this discovery to the attention of the coach. Wouldn't it be utterly amazing if the coach were to say to the players, "Well, there are no goals in here. Guess we'll just have to play tonight's game without 'em."

What if a similar situation occurred on the football field? No goals?

What if the coach were to say, "We'll play without the goals?"

What nonsense.

It would be unimaginable for a team to play basketball or football without some goals. Something has to be achieved. Something has to be accomplished. The goals are the points for the points. Without goals, the games are not.

In life, we can't play the game without the goals. We don't move forward without goals, for no one would be able to discern which way forward is, and if we do not move forward in life, we will discover that, as time passes, we are left in the past. The present and the future belong to those who are headed toward the goal.

There is no achievement in life without goals, for achievement presupposes that there be something to be achieved. That *something* is the goal. It is the target that identifies achievement.

We can't score points nor win victories without goals. Points are the point. That's the way it is.

This aiming thing should not seem strange to us because life is full of goal choosing, preparing for goal reaching, aiming at goals, and determining by evaluation or experience or both whether we scored points. All of us are involved with goals every day of our lives. They might not be as clear as they should be, but we are constantly aiming at goals of one quality or another. Some goal is there for whatever you do. That's inescapable. Some aim is there. You and I are going for something. Our task is to sort out the goal so that we can know for sure what we are aiming at and determining why we want to go for it and ascertaining what it is going to take for us to get there.

A man had not had the benefit of much education, but he knew the area he lived in like the back of his hand. One day when he was asked for directions, he said to a driver, "Go to the creek up yonder and turn left."

The driver asked, "Where's the creek?"

To that question, the fellow who was giving the directions said, "If you weren't know where the creek is, you weren't know nothin'."

Without knowing what your goal is, you're in the same boat.

I haven't done it in a long time, but when I was younger, I loved to go quail hunting.

It was very challenging to me primarily because quail fly fast, and it doesn't take them long to get up to speed. They go from zero to zoom in a hurry. They sit on the ground with their engines running, and when they fly up from there, they do so in great haste.

They get into groups called *coveys*. I like to call them a bird herd. No matter how many birds there are in a covey, generally, when they fly, they stay fairly close together and the covey looks like a swiftly moving blur.

When I first tried to bag some quail, I tried to get the whole bunch or as many as I could by shooting right into the middle of the covey. I knew that I could surely get several birds with one shot, if not every one of them. It looked so easy. I was convinced there was no way I could miss. Not so. Not only did I miss getting the entire covey or a major part thereof, I missed getting even one bird, and it happened more times than seemed fair to me. Foolishly, I kept trying the same thing, and it just wouldn't work. I couldn't even luck out and get any.

An experienced hunter sensed my predicament and suggested to me that I pick out one bird just as soon as the covey flew up. He said, "Don't look at the entire covey. Look for just one bird; concentrate on that one, and see if your luck changes." Guess what. I began to be moderately successful. Dealing with one instead of the whole bunch made a huge difference.

I don't hunt quail any more, but the lesson I learned from my teenage hunting experiences has served me well in life.

In life, we can't aim at everything. We have to focus. We simply can't be successful if we aim at everything in general and nothing in particular.

"Why are you doing all those examinations, doc?" I asked.

The doc said, "I'm trying to find out what's wrong with you."

I asked, "Why don't you skip all those procedures and just treat me for everything?"

Do you think my suggestion was foolish? The doctor did too. He knew that I could hardly afford one ailment, let alone all of them.

The doc was doing the tests because he was looking for *the* problem, and when he found *it*, he would treat *it* and cure *it*.

The parallel to life is obvious. The best way to accomplish nothing is to aim at everything. We have to identify, to isolate, to clarify, to prepare, to overcome obstacles, to aim, to reach, and then to tally the score.

It is important to mention here that as necessary as goals are in our lives, there is nothing sacred about goals *per se*. Some goals, by the very nature of the case, are atrocious. To be worth attaining, goals must be worthy of attaining. They should be honorable and wholesome and pure. Worthy!

In Louisiana I studied with a professor who was the wisest teacher I ever had. He was a lesson more profound than any lesson he ever taught.

One day he told us students about a trip he took on a paddle boat down the Mississippi River from St. Louis to New Orleans.

On one evening of the trip, the darkness was almost palpable and the fog was intensely heavy. The professor said he thought the boat was traveling a bit too fast for conditions, so he went to the captain and talked to him about the darkness and the fog and his concern about the boat's speed. He asked the captain if he knew where all the roots, stumps, and logs in the river were. The captain said that he didn't. My professor said that his heart went up into his throat because he just knew that sooner or later the boat would be ripped on the bottom by one of those roots, stumps, or logs.

The professor said that the captain smiled graciously and said, "Sir, I don't know where all the roots, stumps, or logs in this river are, but I know where the channel is."

The wise teacher then applied the lesson of the story, and what a lesson about life there is in it.

He said, "In life, never mind the roots or the stumps or the logs. Just keep the boat of your life in the channel. Keep your eyes on the channel. Stay on course. Know where the channel is, and keep yourself in it."

That lesson, that one lesson, was worth all the time I spent in college. If I learned nothing else, my college time would have been well spent.

The last thing that wise teacher said to our class that day fastened itself to my mind for my lifetime: "Greatness has direction; it has concentration; it has specific knowledge." He was correct then; he still is. What a teacher!

No matter what you need to do or want to do, the goal is what defines your success or failure. Please remember, *Greatness has direction*.

Good livers aim as high as they realistically can. They set their goals; they give to the realization of their objectives the very best they have. How could any more be demanded or required?

Life is Attempting

There are no worthless people, but there are some useless ones. I don't mean that they are of no use, but useless in the sense that they choose to refuse to use the resources that are available to them. They are the ones whose favorite word is *if*. They rationalize their uselessness by forevermore talking about all the great wonders they would accomplish "if." They say things like, "If we had more time;" "If we had more money;" "If we had better opportunities;" "If it weren't for our circumstances;" "If it weren't for our sorry neighbors;" "If it weren't for the governments;" "If we had been educated better;" "If we had better customers;" "If we only had better employees;" "If it weren't for my boss;" "If things didn't cost so much;" "If folks understood us better." Incessantly those *iffers* rattle on.

I don't believe what they say about the *if* stuff. Folks who are not doing their best right now wouldn't be doing their best no matter what they had. If they had more of what they think they need and less of what they think they don't need, chances are extremely good they still would not do their best with it. A wise man said to me, "If a frog had pockets, he'd wear pistols so he could shoot snakes." It's not a matter of ability or capability. It's a matter of adaptability and usability. Our best doesn't depend upon, "If we had that;" it depends upon, "Since we have this."

Tom and John, two college guys, both had dates one night. Tom returned to the dorm about midnight. John, dirty, greasy, sweaty, and utterly worn out, got in about 1:30 A.M.

When John arrived, Tom asked him, "What in the world happened to you?"

John answered, "My girl and I were riding along, and she said, 'I feel so romantic. If you would stop and let the top to this car down, I believe I could just melt in your arms.'"

Tom said, "My girl said the same thing to me, so I did and she did, but I didn't come back to the dorm at 1:30 in the morning in the condition you're in."

John said, "Yeah, but you've got a convertible."

There's something to be said for people who do the best they can with what they have in whatever circumstances they find themselves. Here's to you, John.

We show what we are by what we do with what we have.

There is something special about the cowboy who was observed wearing only one spur and was asked, "Why are you wearing just one spur?"

The cowboy said, "Well, I feel like if I get one side of my horse going, the other side will come on."

I love folks like him who don't complain about not having more to do with. They put to good and sensible use what they have. They use whatever they have.

The good livers don't whine and pine and moan and groan about what they don't have and what they can't do. What do they do instead? They assess what they have. They resourcefully and creatively put it to work, and they are as happy as can be with the results. They hold their heads up because they know they have done all they could do with what they had in the circumstances in which they did it. Good livers know they don't have the goods to do everything, but they know they have enough to do something.

A preacher had been visiting a family. When he started to leave, his car wouldn't start. He got out of the car, raised the hood, bent forward underneath the hood looking at the engine as if he knew what he was looking for. I suppose he did that because he had seen folks beside the road with disabled cars with the hoods up doing the same thing. He thought what he was doing was what one is supposed to do when his car won't start.

After briefly looking around under the hood, he stood up, and when he did, the hood latch caught the crown of his head and nearly knocked him out. He grabbed his head with both hands as he writhed in agonizing pain.

A passerby saw the good reverend clutching his head, stopped, got out of his car, and ran over to the man of the cloth.

He asked, "What happened, preacher?"

The preacher yelled out, "I hit my head on that hood latch, and I think I'm gonna die."

The fellow asked, "Did you cuss?"

In a raspy voice, the preacher said, "No, but if you'll write it down, I'll sign it."

That's what you call doing your best under the circumstances. We have to use what we have and make the best of it.

We can't wait until all the questions are answered or until all the problems are solved or until all the uncertainties are resolved. We can't wait until we can do things to perfection. Procrastination won't work. Inertia will hurt'cha. We must use what we have and use it now. Life is attempting, not avoiding.

A farmer, already worn out from his hard day's work, went out to his barn to milk his cow. When he got to the stall, he pulled up his milking stool and flopped down on it. The cow looked around at him, and said, "John, are you tired?"

The farmer replied, "Bossie, I'm so tired I can hardly stand it."

She asked, "Are you too tired to milk?"

John said, "I believe I am."

The cow said, "Well, just grab hold, and I'll jump up and down."

Thanks, Bossie, for teaching us the lessons of adaptability and constructive action.

Two cows were standing side by side with their heads pointing in the same direction. Flies were awful that day, but the cows had a resourceful way to deal with the pestering problem. Standing in their positions, they swished their tails in opposite directions, thus keeping the flies off each other.

You can call it *cooperation* or *cow-operation*, but in either case, they were getting the job done using what they had, and they were doing it with half the effort. Talk about efficiency. They were doing the necessary task, and they were doing it right. There was no operational error in their performance.

Use what you have, or you won't have it long. If you stall, you'll fall; if you stop, you'll drop. *Making it* lies in the effort, in the attempt. Like muscles, our resources are strengthened with use.

The good livers somehow manage to adapt to the climate. They have their opportunities, and they seize them. They have their resources, and they use them. They have their time, and they invest it.

When it comes to the business of using one's resources and time and opportunities there are two kinds of people: those who are glad they did and those who wish they had. Life is using, not excusing. It is trying, not sighing. It is lifting, not folding.

We all make mistakes, but they should not keep us from trying again some other way. Our blunders have extraordinary educational value. There's hardly a better teacher than a first-class mistake, because we learn more from our mistakes than we learn in almost any other way.

I remember taking an exam in an English class. There were ten questions on it. I knew nine of them inside out. The other one was a mystery.

After the tests were returned to us, I discussed my paper with the professor. I said, "I couldn't come up with an answer for number seven."

She said, "And you did so well with the other nine."

I couldn't remember the answers to those nine questions that I aced if I were threatened with hemorrhoid surgery, but to this day I remember the correct answer to the one I missed.

So what if we miss a few things along the way? So what if we make a mistake now and then? Once we get it right, we'll know it from then on. Do the best you can with what you have now; the mistakes can be dealt with later.

Some of the comments television and radio folks say during ball games amaze me. I heard one say several times during a game when passes were not completed, "The quarterback should not have thrown that pass. He was lucky that throw was not intercepted." He would say, "That was a ball that never should have been thrown." I guess the folks who comment as a game is being played have to say *something*, so they do.

When I hear comments about pass plays that were bad or never should have been attempted, my comment to the commentator is; "I suppose the only pass that should have been thrown is the completed one." Now would-n't that just be ideal? How in the world can one tell if a pass will be completed or not unless it's attempted? It doesn't make a heck of a lot of sense to me to say that something should not have been done because it failed. How do you know if you don't try? It might succeed. It might work. It might turn out to have been the right move.

Everything we do does not succeed. Everything doesn't always work out the way we hoped for. How can anyone say we shouldn't have tried?

You can be sure you won't mess up if you don't try anything, but you will not know what you can do until you try. When a forward pass is attempted, three things can happen, and, for the offensive team, two of them are bad, but one of them is good. Why not take a chance on the good thing? The team will never know how good a thing can be unless they throw the ball.

Do the best you can with what you have and watch what happens. The results might happily be what you've been wanting all the time.

Someone asked me, "What do you want your epitaph to be?"

That's a sobering question. I had never really thought about it, so I gave it some thought so that I could answer as intelligently and as seriously as I could. I would have joked about it and said, "I would like for it to be not for as long as I can help it," but I could tell the questioner was serious.

I said, "I would like it to say, 'With what he had, he did his best.'" I said that to him because I firmly believe that nothing is good enough unless it *is* good enough. If I am eating a pizza or making a speech, I want to do my best.

This matter of using one's resources and abilities and opportunities in order to be one's best requires a great deal of concentration, awareness, discipline, and self-respect. To say the least, it's not easy because, if we don't watch out, we can become satisfied with where we are and what we are doing and how well we are doing it. We can talk ourselves into believing that we *are* good enough. We can talk ourselves right into a comfort zone telling ourselves, "We have arrived."

There's a problem with that kind of thinking, however. It's a difficult thing to hold our own. If we are not progressing, we are regressing. It's deceptively easy to get into a rut, and the rut route is a bad way to travel, for when we become satisfied, we go backwards because we tend to do less than we did before we became satisfied with ourselves.

It's so easy for all of us to fall into the trap of sacrificing the best for the good. All it would take to be our best is just a little more time, a little more discipline, a little more attention to the task, and some more self-respect. We don't have to surrender to sorrow nor capitulate to complacency nor acquiesce to the average. Life can be better than that.

The very act of doing our best motivates us to improve even more. Excellent performance encourages us to do even better the next time. Excellence in anything motivates us to seek ways to make our best better.

Excellence is habit forming. The fact that we yearn for more must mean that there is more for us to be.

This business of being resourceful and adapting and attempting and being creative and doing the best you can with what you have is important stuff, and it will cause you to be a better liver of life if you do it. It won't work, on the other hand, if you merely intend to do it, but never get around to it.

If you agree with the notion that it would be useful for you to use your resources but respond with good intentions only, you are no better off than before. Good intentions, abiding alone, never stirring anyone to constructive action, are worse than useless. Intentions make good inventions only when the intentions are coupled with intelligent implementation. *Intention* and *indolence* are too close for comfort; therefore, let's get the ice out of our hearts, the lead out of our feet, and the cobwebs out of our brains, and let's get on with it. There's nothing commending about intending.

It would be tragic for you to have seen your potential but not to have strived for it; for you to have had many opportunities but not to have seized them; for you to have known the way but not to have taken it; for you to have had dreams but not to have followed them; for you to have seen the prize but not to have reached for it; for you to have had in your hands the resources of successful life but not to have used them.

A lady and her five-year-old daughter were in a variety store. The little girl wandered away from her mother and found the candy counter. She walked from one end of the counter to the other, looking carefully at the various candies.

When her mother finished shopping, she said, "Time to go home. Come on."

The little girl seemed not to hear, for she kept walking, looking at the candies.

Her mother patiently waited a little while, then insisted, "Come on, now. We have to go home."

Her daughter stopped, looked at her mother, and said, "Mama, you gave me just a nickel. I want to be sure I spend it right."

We get only one chance at life. We have one life to live, one life to use. Good livers make a concentrated effort to *spend it right*.

Life is Seeing

A young doctor went into practice with his dad who had been practicing old-time country medicine for several years. The first day of the joint practice, both doctors went out into the countryside to make some house calls. Dr. Dad advised his son, "Practicing medicine out here is not the way it is in the city. It's a different ball game out here. You really have to observe. You have to pay attention to the most minute details. Every little thing is important. To show you what I'm talking about, I will take care of the first two patients, and you can see how I handle them so you'll know what it takes to be a country doctor."

After examining the first patient, Dr. Dad said, "Mr. C., you've got to quit smoking. You have no choice. You're going to kill yourself with your smoking. You have to quit right now."

When both doctors walked outside, Dr. Son asked, "How did you know about his smoking?"

Dr. Dad replied, "Didn't you see all those cigarette butts lying around? I told you before, 'You've got to observe. You have to pay attention to the details.'"

They went on to the next patient's house. Dr. Dad said, "Observe carefully this time."

After examining the patient, Dr. Dad said, "Mr. B., you've got to quit drinking so much. It'll kill you if you don't. You must give it up."

When they walked outside, Dr. Son asked, "How did you know about his drinking?"

Dr. Dad said, "Didn't you see those beer cans and liquor bottles in the trash can? I'm telling you, you've got to observe with these patients out here."

Dr. Dad continued, "All right, now, let's see if you're ready. You take the next patient, and I'll see if you've got it."

Following the examination, Dr. Son said, "Ms. H., you're going overboard on your religion. You need to slow down on that religion thing. It's going to be too bad for you if you don't."

When they walked outside, Dr. Dad, perplexed beyond all measure, asked Dr. Son, "How in heaven's name did you know about her going overboard on her religion?"

Dr. Son said, "Dad, didn't you observe? Didn't you see that preacher's head sticking out from under the foot of the bed?"

Important to observe, isn't it?

Let's see what we can see about seeing.

A family was having a family reunion, an event at which all the family, the in-laws, the grands, the cousins, the aunts, the uncles, the nephews, the children, the grandparents, all the kin get together to do a lot of eating and just to see one another. We like to do stuff like that here in the South.

After the big feed, some of the family noticed that Grandpa was not around. They looked for him all over the place, but he couldn't be found. Nobody knew it, but Grandpa had gotten into some booze and was somewhat inebriated. Really, he was flat drunk.

Somehow he had wound up in a hog pen. The family finally found him lying there with one of his arms draped over a big sow.

Walking up to the pen, the family members heard Grandpa with a drunken voice say to the hog, "You know what, wife, I've been married to you for forty years, and this is the first time I ever noticed that you had two rows of buttons on your gown."

How refreshing it is to notice things. If we looked around a bit more, there's no telling what we would see.

We need to take the time to really see things, to be aware. Life is seeing. It's noticing. It's observing. It's catching what we would miss if we didn't look.

All of us need to work on heightening our awareness of everything around us. We miss so much because we don't look with the intention of seeing. It's not that there's nothing to see, but we are blinded by the obvious. It's there all right, but we have a knack for missing it.

I saw a friend of mine working on his lawn mower. He didn't appear to be working too hard, so I went over to chat with him for a while.

His son, eager to get on with his summer yard mowing work, was waiting for his daddy to get the mower repaired.

His dad said, "Son, go to the barn and get the pliers. They're in that tool box on the top shelf."

His son was gone about forty-five seconds. When he came back, he said, "I can't find 'em."

His dad said, "Well, go look again. I know they're in that tool box. Look good this time."

It wasn't long until his son came back with the pliers.

Have you ever looked for something that was right there, but you didn't see it? Did you ever go back and *look good this time*?

Don't you think we need to do more *looking* in life? Wouldn't life be much richer and more enjoyable if we were more aware of our surroundings so that we could really see them, so that we could really notice them, so that we could really look at them, so that we could really observe them?

A farmer knew some of his cows weren't in the pasture where they were supposed to be, so he asked his ten-year-old son to go look for them. The son was gone about five minutes. When he came back toward the house, his dad said, "Find 'em?"

His son said, "No, sir."

His dad said, "You sure weren't gone very long. Where'd you look?"

The son said, "I went to the end of the lane and scattered all over everywhere."

Often our attention is just like that. We go to the end of the lane and *scatter*. Has your attention ever been like that? We have so much to do, so much to keep up with, so much to think about. Too much I think. Oh, yes, we might be somewhat aware, but every now and then we become victims of a scattered, unfocused awareness. Have you ever had your awareness wander away?

Reality, I know, is not adjustable, but *we* are. Reality is always all there, but sometimes we aren't. We become preoccupied, so we miss things. Every now and then someone will tell me, "I came close to having an accident awhile ago. I went right through a stop sign. I just didn't see it. I guess I was thinking about something besides driving. I wasn't paying close enough attention to what I was doing."

Preoccupation is not always dangerous, but it is often enough the reason for our being unaware of our surroundings.

Another reason for our not seeing is that we aren't interested in what's going on. We see the light; we know it's there, but for the time being, we're not interested enough to pay any real attention.

Sometimes we don't see things because we really don't care about them one way or the other. We just don't give a hum about 'em.

A farmer bought a mule so he could get his spring plowing done. He got the mule home, hitched him up, and started plowing. When the mule reached the end of the row, instead of turning to the right or to the left, as any good mule should do, he walked smack-dab into the fence. He did it twice. The first time the farmer didn't think much about it, but the second time the farmer concluded, "I've bought a mule that can't see."

He took the mule back to the man he had bought the mule from and said, "This mule walked into my fence twice. He wouldn't stop to turn around. He tore my fence up in two places. I figure he can't see."

The former owner of the mule said, "Naw, he can see all right. He just don't give a flip."

Did you ever know anybody like that mule? Indifferent? Didn't care? Didn't "give a flip?"

That kind of attitude will sure enough keep someone from seeing things, won't it? How can one go about the task of getting indifferent folks to open the eyes of their minds and their souls? I don't know what the answer is, but I do know that it's exceedingly difficult to deal with folks who *don't give a flip*.

Whether it's preoccupation or a lack of interest or indifference or something else, all of us at times can be blinded by the obvious. We get so used to it that we don't see it anymore.

Isn't it time for us to back up, to take another look and to start savoring what we've been skipping? We'd better mind things or we'll miss 'em. Let's start taking notice. Let's *see* now. Let's start admitting into our minds more of the stuff of life, and let's hold onto it for closer observation.

As with anything else in life that is worthwhile, getting good at this awareness thing takes work. It's sort of easy to let it slide what with everything else we've got to do. It takes concentration to get into the groove of noticing the things of life, but after some practice, it becomes habitual. So, if you lay hold of awareness, before long it will lay hold of you. It would probably be a good idea not to wait long to get started on it.

Awareness is part of what I mean when I say, "Life is seeing." Anyone and everyone can and should become more aware of life's surroundings. That's not all there is to it, though.

Becoming aware might involve change for you. If it does, then make the change gracefully. You'll be glad you did.

The changes that we make in our lives are the results of our becoming aware of circumstances suggesting or requiring change. We wouldn't change anything unless we became aware of a need to change it. To change for any other reason would be to change merely for its own sake. I'm not talking about that kind of change; I'm talking about change that is needed. To change without an awareness of need would be like learning to swim before you get into the water or like coming back from somewhere you haven't been. We change, we adjust, we modify as we become aware of need. Need sparks thought, and we change as our thinking changes.

In my neck of the woods, *takes after* is a term used by folks to refer to the way children look like or act like their parents, or, at least one or the other of their parents. If a daughter looks like her mother, she *takes after* her mother. If a son has ways like his daddy, he *takes after* his daddy.

Our behavior *takes after* our thinking. Wherever our thoughts go, our actions will follow; therefore, when our thoughts change, our lives change with them. When our thinking and our wills change, a change in what we do is not far behind.

Need stimulates thought, and thought initiates behavior so the way to change whatever needs changing is to change our minds about it. You and I will be as unmoved as a patient under anesthesia until we sense a need to change. Our *no* or our *go* depends on our awareness of need.

I was trying as hard as I could to catch some fish. I was having no luck at all. No nibbles; no fish.

I thought, *I was here just a few days ago, and I caught the limit in an hour. Now this? I am doing everything today exactly as I did the last time. What's the problem?*

I became aware of a fellow about fifty yards in front of me pulling in fish so fast he was about to wear a hole in the water.

I yelled at him, "What bait you usin'?"

He told me.

Not having any of that kind of bait with me, I paddled to the dock, went to the bait stand, got some bait, went back to my spot, hooked on the bait, put it into the water, and before long I had the limit.

I could have responded differently when I became aware that guy was catching fish. I could have criticized his bait. I could have said to myself, *I've never heard of anybody catching fish in this lake with that bait. That guy must not know much about fishin'. I'll bet he doesn't know a crappie from a cabbage.*

I didn't think any of that. It never occurred to me to criticize him.

He was catching fish, and, if what he told me was true, he was doing it with that bait. I saw him doing it.

I figured if he could do it, so could I. He was and I could and I did.

I'm not too proud to change when I become aware that I need to. Are you?

I'm glad I was paying attention that day. Awareness can make a difference in our lives in ways that are a heck of a lot more important than catching or not catching fish.

Another important aspect of this seeing thing is vision.

Vision means much more than seeing what is present to the eyes. In a broader application, vision refers to seeing *into* things; therefore, it is insight and it is foresight because it is prospective as well as introspective. Folks who have this vision ability can see far more than whatever they're looking at, for their *sight* reaches out from and beyond what their eyes can see. It is a seeing with the eyes of the mind and of the soul; and it is the kind of seeing everybody can do, for it resides in the realm of ideas, and, when it is finished, it generates implementation.

Vision is one's ability to see more than what is seen, to see beyond what is seen, and to see it while there is still time. It is kin to imagination. It is a process of intellect and emotion. It is the product of the head-heart team. When you hear folks talking about their dreams or their aspirations, they are talking about what I mean by the word *vision*. Vision takes into account what is, but it goes deeper. It sees what can be. It is a forward-seeing kind of seeing. Vision is a thought-out, dwelled-on, planned-for, achievable expectation. It is *looking out* and a *looking forth*. It is a mind-stretching, faith-built exercise. It is what moves us from here to there with eager anticipation.

People who have done anything worthwhile in life have been moved by vision. They had dreams, goals, hopes, ideas, concepts, something they *saw* as worthy of achievement, something which could be transformed into concrete reality.

When you have vision, you see from the beginning a form of the end. People who get things done are inspired by vision. They are not visionary; they are people of vision. *Vision* and *visionary* are a chasm apart. *Vision* is healthy; *visionary* is not. *Vision* things are realistic; *visionary* things are impractical.

When motivational writers or speakers write or talk about *thinking big* and *planning big* and *being more* and *attempting greater things* and *realizing your potential* and similar phases, they are talking about the power of vision. They might discuss all those ideas under different headings, but what they are doing is encouraging us to exercise the eyes of our minds and to act positively and courageously upon what we see. What they tell us about that approach is right, of course. What it all boils down to is this: vision is crucial to victory.

Vision begets creativity. It inspires us, redirecting our attention and energy, creating involvement. It gets things done, gets us stimulated, stirred and started, bearing us along on its powerful wings. It is the springboard of invention, discovery, and success.

People of vision are not only movers, they inspire others to become movers, too. They help other folks break loose from a mediocre, business-as-usual attitude and break forth to a life that is extraordinary and wonderful. Great leaders do that particularly well because their sense of vision is so keen.

The good livers do their best to see all that life has for them.

They look at the past to review their successes and their failures. They look at their successes to reaffirm to themselves how those successes contributed to their sense of confidence and competence in the present. They survey their failures and from them determine what they learned about life that didn't work so that now they can apply the successful ideas more intelligently.

The good livers, furthermore, look to the future with realistic optimism and hope, driven by their visions of what they and the people around them can become. They don't chase mirages, mind you, but they do follow their dreams.

Well, how does this seeing thing look to you? What do you want? What are you interested in? What do you take time to look at? What about your ideas? I'll bet a lot of them are worth looking into. Why not get some start into your heart and let your vision lead you on to bigger and better things? Why not?

My throat was sore. I went to see my doctor. When he came into the room, he asked, "What can I do for you, Wayne?"

I told him about my throat.

He got his light and a wooden stick and told me to open my mouth. I guess he figured I didn't know where my throat was.

He said, "O.K., throat, let me have a look at you."

While he was looking, I was thinking. He was too, but he was thinking, *There's a forty-dollar throat if I ever saw one.*

I was thinking about life. That's what I do most of the time anyway.

I was thinking, *Life, let me have a look at you. Let me start right now looking at you and the wonders of you as I never have before. Life, let me get to know you better. Let me observe you more closely. Let me explore your dimensions. Life, I want to become aware of you. I want to dream of all that you and I together can become. I want to savor every minute that I have with you.*

I hope that you will join me in that kind of adventure so that both of us can realize to the fullest what it means to say, *Life is seeing.*

O.K., life, let me have a look at you.

Tantalizing, isn't it?

Life is Enthusiasm-ing

The parents wanted their five-year-old son to memorize some Bible verses to recite at church.

One of the verses on their list was one that says, "Many are called, but few are chosen."

The parents worked with the little guy until they were sure he had committed all the verses to memory.

When the time came for the recitation at church, the child was up front and all ready to do his thing. The parents were filled with eager anticipation and with pride.

When he got to the verse, "Many are called, but few are chosen," he became confused and said, "Many are cold, and a few are frozen."

His parents became rigid with embarrassment. The kid smiled proudly, for he thought he had it right.

He misquoted the verse, yes, but he had no idea how right he was. He got a very important truth exactly right.

There are a bunch of those *frozen* folks around. Their defroster is out of order. You couldn't de-ice them on hot asphalt. You couldn't budge them with a crowbar. It's awful to be around people who are not excited about life. If you don't watch out, their iciness will take the wind right out of your sails.

Someone asked a country preacher, "What do you preach about most of the time?"

He replied, "I preach on love and faith and fellowship and things like that."

The questioner asked, "Why don't you preach on lying and adultery and drinking liquor and cussing and things like that?"

The preacher responded, "I tried that one time and an awful coldness came over the meeting."

A coldness comes *over the meeting* when I am in the presence of folks who are not enthusiastic about life. Their temperature for life is so low I can feel the frost coming on. It's indescribably uncomfortable for me.

On the other hand, people who are warmhearted and enthusiastic are uplifting and exciting to be with. They have life in their lives, and they aren't too dignified to show it. It's great.

Enthusiasm is to life what wind is to a sail; what belief is to motivation; what inspiration is to invention; what practice is to perfection; what knowledge is to understanding. It is that indispensable dynamic that makes life come alive.

Life is too large, too marvelous, too majestic, too miraculous to be crammed into a program of coldness, indifference, mediocrity, or nonchalant complacency. It's terrible to be uninspired or uninspiring.

I heard a speaker tell a group, "When I die and when you hear about it, you can truthfully say, 'Well, that's the first time he's been dead, ain't it?'

I want to be just like that. I don't want to act as if I'm dead. I don't want to be like it, talk like it, walk like it, look like it, work like it, laugh like it, nor live like it. I don't want any apathy nor atrophy to have anything to do with me. Lethargy, dullness, dreariness, depression, drabness, or boredom are not for me. I hope I'm never plagued with any of them.

A lack of passion for life is not beneath my dignity; it is above my dignity. I'm not too dignified to be excited about life. I hope I never get so dignified that my heart shrivels to feelinglessness. Dignity is all right in its place, but if that place carries you beyond enthusiasm, you're too high.

I want some heat in my heart, some spark in my spirit. I want the band to strike up every day of my life. It's good to keep the lights brightly shining. How about you?

Enthusiasm puts the dream into the dreamer, and the talk into the talker, and the auction into the auctioneer, and the drive into the driver, and the farm into the farmer, and the propel into the propeller, and the heat into the heater, and the start into the starter, and the bat into the battery, and the edge into education, and the sell into the seller, and the lead into the leader, and the work into the worker, and the sing into the singer, and the engine into the engineer, and the give into the giver, and the magnet into magnetism, and the compute into the computer, and the preach into the preacher, and the teach into the teacher, and the super into the supervisor, and the write into the writer, and the speak into the speaker, and the awe into the audience. Enthusiasm puts the vital into vitality, and the urge into urgency. It turns scraps into scrappers, the dead into the dynamic, and the indolent into the industrious. It puts the live into the liver.

Enthusiasm is heat, yes, but it's also light. A pilot said to me, "I don't take off in the fog." That's a good practice for a pilot, especially if he or she is flying with visual flight rules. It's also a good practice for the enthusiastic liver. Don't *take off in the fog*. Beware of zeal that is not according to knowledge. Be enthusiastic, but don't get carried away. Don't overdo it. Balance is always healthy.

Sometimes on a farm, dry weather is needed, but a drought can be devastating. Sometimes rain is helpful, but a flood can put a farmer out of business. Enthusiasm is good, but too much can overheat the engine. Enthusiasm is not a frenzied fit. It is an excited mind and heart that are under control. A man once told me that, "Folks should be as energetic as a dentist's drill, but just as controlled." That's an excellent way to put it. Why didn't I think of that? That's exactly what enthusiasm is. Energy under control.

Furthermore, enthusiasm is energetic intelligence. Uninformed enthusiasm becomes foolish blindness, and it spells trouble. It is emotion only, and it can be dangerous.

To be enthusiastic doesn't mean that your intellect stays in the freezer. It helps to have some knowledge in the kettle. The kettle will blow just as much steam as one that contains no knowledge, and it will just know what to do with it.

It's good to be enthusiastic, but it's bad to have enthusiasm to the extent that common sense is dismissed. No sense can be made of not taking common sense into account. Intelligent, enlightened, informed, elucidated common sense is powerful, and it's always in season.

The high school football coach had tried everything he could think of to get his team to score. Nothing had worked. He called his last time-out with forty seconds left in the game. The score was 7-6 in favor of the opposing team. The coach was frantic. During the time-out, he called over to him a ninth grade quarterback who had never been in a regular game. The kid was excited that the coach called his name. He ran up to the coach. The coach said, "I'm going to put you into the game. Can you follow my instructions?"

The player excitedly said, "Yes, Sir, I can."

The coach said, "Here's what we're gonna do. I want you to run two quarterback sneaks, and on third down, quick kick, and maybe we'll get a fumble recovery in the end zone and get a touchdown. We've got to get a score. You got that now?"

The young quarterback said, "Yes, Sir. I've got it. Two quarterback sneaks, then quick kick."

The coach said, "Right. Now do what I told you."

The quarterback hustled out onto the field. He was so excited he could hardly contain himself.

On the first play, he ran the quarterback sneak for a thirty-yard gain. The clock kept running. On the second down, he ran a quarterback sneak. He gained yardage down to the one foot line where a defensive player made a shoestring tackle. The clock kept running. The young quarterback's coach was about to have a nervous collapse. On third down, the ninth-grader received the football from the center, backed up about ten yards, and kicked the ball over the fence into the parking lot. The clock ran out as the team and the coach were shocked with disbelief.

As fast as he could run, the coach raced up to his young quarterback and screamed at him, "What in the world is the matter with you? What were you thinking?"

The young player said, "Coach, all I could think of was that you sure do call dumb plays."

You know, whatever you're doing and however excited you are about it, it's a good idea to take with you a generous supply of common sense.

We can forgive the football player for what he did. After all, he was following instructions, and the pressure was enormous.

For you and me, however, even if we do get in the pressure cooker from time to time, don't forget to carry along a good supply of common sense.

Returning home from a speaking engagement not long ago, traveling southbound on I-75, I had my CB radio on, listening to some truck drivers talking. I enjoy listening to 'em because I learn a lot from their down-home wisdom. The truckers don't talk to me much, not that I don't have any down-home wisdom, but they know as soon as I say a word that I'm not a *driver*, so they don't say a whole lot to me. They're polite, of course, but they prefer to talk to folks who speak and understand the truckers' special language, much of which is unintelligible to me. At any rate, there were three big trucks just ahead of me, and the drivers were carrying on a conversation as they rode along. I was close enough for my radio to pick up their transmissions clearly.

In the distance, however, I could hear two other truckers talking. One of them was really angry about something. I couldn't pick up the conversation clearly, but I could make out enough to tell that he was super mad. The drivers right in front of me heard the two arguing also because they made comments about the *arguin'* going on between *them two drivers*.

In a little while, one of the arguing drivers said to the other one, "Pull over and stop and I'll get up there where you are and I'll beat the daylights outta you." He didn't actually say *daylights*, but it wouldn't be good for me to use the same word he used.

One of the drivers in a truck just ahead of me heard the threat, and said, "You know, I did that same thing one time. I got to arguin' with a driver, and I told him to pull over and I'd come up there and beat the *daylights* outta him." He went on, "He stopped, and I went up to where he was, and it seemed to me like it took him thirty minutes to unroll outta that truck. He was a big, big man. He finally got out and me and him went to it, and he beat me so bad that when he got through whippin' me, I told him I never had anybody to whip me so bad." Then he laughed a little and continued, "I even went to a truckstop with him and bought him a cup of coffee. Since then I ain't never told nobody that I'd whip him before I had a chance to see him first."

The point? Don't get carried away. Enthusiasm, yes, but don't forget that valuable beyond calculation is the companionship of common sense. Take it with you wherever you go.

Rev. Claude Fullerton is a retired Methodist preacher from Cordele, Georgia. He is a delightful, wise man from whom I have received considerable knowledge and inspiration. During one of our conversations, I said, "Tell me the first thing you think of when I say the word *enthusiasm*."

With a twinkle in his eye, he said, "Can't-wait-itis, excitement. I'm that way about my gardening. I love it, and I just can't wait to get to it. I'm excited about it. I've got a bad case of can't-wait-itis."

As we talked on, he said, "Enthusiasm is interest and joy. Interest generates excitement, and joy is the result of doing what you're enthusiastic about."

Precisely.

Why do folks get excited about jobs, or schools, or classes, or subjects, or other people, or new houses, or new cars, or old cars, or new trucks, or old trucks, or retirement, or ball games, or contests, or pageants, or concerts, or new toys, or vacations, or holidays, or gifts, or guests, or sales, or meetings, or new products, or rose gardens, or vegetable gardens, or pay raises, or pleasant surprises, or huge profits, or new clothes, or graduations, or weddings, or children, or grandchildren, or grandparents, or parents, or new furniture, or whatever excites them? Because they are *interested* in them. That interest fosters excitement and excited involvement engenders joy.

Students are motivated in subjects they're interested in. When students find some subjects dull, it isn't that the subjects are dull in and of themselves, but that the students lack interest in them. Sometimes that circumstance changes because some teachers can be so excited about a *dull* subject that a student catches the spirit of the teacher and a formerly *dull* subject becomes interesting because the teacher is.

On the other hand, a student's interest in a formerly interesting subject can slow down if the teacher is dull. Dull presenters make for dull subjects, I suppose. At any rate, if someone is interested in something, the motivation level is going to be much higher than it would be otherwise; hence, the level of enthusiasm will be higher, too, for enthusiasm is interest.

There's something special about people who are excited about who they are, and what they are, and why they are, and what they're doing, and why they're doing it, and those with whom, and for whom they're doing it. I like the *go-getters*, the *live wires*, the folks who have their *hearts in it*, the ones with the gusto and the zest.

Enthusiasm is the great driver in our lives. It compels us and propels us and impels us, driving us with excitement, interest, and joy.

Enthusiasm also means challenge. There is something stimulating about challenge, about risk. To live without challenge wouldn't be very exciting. Anyone who plays it safe by not attempting much is not going to be very excited about anything. That's a mighty sluggish way to travel. It doesn't take much energy to live an unchallenged life; it's not any fun either. I've never tried it, but I don't see how it could be fun, do you? Taking on the challenge, taking on the risk, taking on the odds fire us up with hope and expectation. That's enthusiasm. It makes us what we are and keeps us from being what we are not.

When we get *pumped* up about a plan or a program or a project or people, there will inevitably be one or more somebody's who will attempt to cool our ardor, to slow us, to calm us down. Such an approach might take the form of discouragement. It could be outright criticism or opposition. It might be silent indifference. In some form, though, the attempt to quench our spirits will come. Enthusiasm has a bunch of enemies, and one or the other of them will come after us.

If we are swayed by them, they can surely dampen our spirits and cause us to lose heart and, ultimately, to fail. I wish it weren't that way, but it is.

To all the attempts to put out our fires, let the voice of our enthusiasm say, *There is too much interest here, too much joy, too much hope, too much expectation. You can't extinguish our fires. They're too big for you. We will win, not you; so, back off and let us through.*

Let there be no diminution; let there be no lasting discouragement; let there be no dimming or dying; let there be no fading and no failing.

Let our enthusiasm prevail.

Enthusiasm is the blood of the spirit, and good livers are not anemic.

Life is Valuing

A couple on a date were playing checkers in a car parked in front of a college dormitory. They must have been playing checkers because a passerby heard the young woman tell the young man, "One more move, and I'll crown you."

Valuing, determining values, is life's crowning move. It is the charger for all the other moves in life. It cuts to the heart of everything we are and everything we do. Determining our standards for our beliefs, for our conduct, and for our character deserves the best and the clearest thought of which we are capable. It is that important.

At one of its meetings a civic group was honored to hear a very distinguished speaker, a highly successful lecturer who spoke to groups all over the country.

During the introduction of the noted speaker, the president of the club said, "In our meetings we have had speakers of high rank and of low rank, but our speaker today is the rankest one we've ever had."

In life, in terms of rank, evaluating is the rankest, for all else depends upon it. Our sense of values guides our every move. It rightfully belongs at the head of the list.

Life is a piece of fine construction. It is composed of foundation, support, utility, and beauty. At its best it is a harmonious and symmetrical unification of all its separate parts. Life's *parts* form a unit, unique and inextricably combined.

Every one of these *parts* revolves around the axis of value. It is one of the *parts*, but it is the central *part*. It is to life what the brain is to the *central* nervous system. Values determine the functions of the other *parts* of life. Values dictate motivation and action. They are the why, the what, the how much, the when, and the where as well as the to what degree of life. Once you have identified your values, you have identified the core, the essence of your life.

It is extremely important, therefore, that we give ourselves to ideas, beliefs, and pursuits that are vitally valuable and permanently profitable. It is not extraordinarily difficult to determine what is really valuable and what is not, what is lasting and what is not, what is important and what is not, what makes life better and what does not. There is nothing mystifying nor enigmatic about it. To be sure, we might not appreciate the distinctions as well as we ought to, but we know the distinctions are there, and we know what they are.

Imagine the confusion. In the days before price scanners in grocery stores, some vandals got into a store one night and changed the prices on many of the marked items. It was really difficult for the employees to get that situation straightened out the next morning. High prices marked on inexpensive items. Low prices marked on more costly items. What a mess.

Assigning high values to cheap items is a trendy approach these days, I think. Not only is there a tendency to assign high value to inferior-value items, but the high quality items have been valued downward.

It does not take an eagle eye to see that there has been a general lowering of value standards in virtually every area of life which has been accompanied by a compromising acceptance of such decline. Everyone is not a standard lowerer nor a compromiser, but it is true generally. Most folks want other folks to accept them, and the way to do that is to be like everybody else. Conformity with low quality values is a rampant problem nowadays.

Concomitant with a general lowering of value standards along with a general spirit of compromise with such a decline, is the applause that compromise receives and the ridicule that is heaped upon those who want to maintain high standards. I have not talked to anyone who sees much prospect for a turnaround in this downward spiral.

I asked one man in particular about this concern of mine. He is a man of years and of letters. He is a man of understanding and compassion. I respect him highly, so I sought his opinion. I asked, "Do you see any prospect for a return to high value standards in modern life?"

He said, "I surely hope there will be."

I repeated, "Do you see any prospect?"

He said, "It doesn't look like there will be any such return."

I am not a pessimist about things, but this values issue has me concerned.

What has happened? What has precipitated the decline in value standards?

The difference between appearance and reality has become blurred. This, of course, did not have to happen. It was not by necessity. There was nothing that I know of that forced them to become blurred. We allowed it to happen, and that condition can throw a value system into disarray in a hurry. This blurred vision has caused many of us to see what is not there and not to see what is there.

The guy thought the woman he had married was authentically beautiful, but he discovered that her hair was a wig, that her eyelashes were false, that her complexion was paint, and that her figure was held in place by a triple-strength harness. He saw what was not and did not see what was. Values are affected by the same kind of distorted perception.

A traveling preacher was spending the night with a family who lived in a rural area. The family had six children, and the youngest of them, a boy of six years, thought that the preacher was one of the finest fellows in the world. The preacher took up a lot of time with the kid, telling him stories and reading to him. They became good friends.

An hour or so after supper, it was time for everybody to go to bed. The children all went to bed before the grown folks did.

When the preacher was walking toward his room, he stopped to tell his young friend good night. As he opened the door slightly, all he could see was the youngster's head above the bed. The preacher thought, *He's kneeling by his bed saying his prayers*, so he quietly knelt by the bed opposite the side where the child was, and he began to pray silently.

The young guy said to the preacher, "What are you doin'?"

The preacher said, "I'm doing the same thing you're doing."

The youngster said, "I'm gonna tell my mama, and she's gonna be real mad."

The preacher asked, "Why will she be mad?"

The little fellow replied, "Because there's just one pot in this room, and I've got it."

Things are not always what they seem to be.

The beautiful bright blue light in the bug killing device hanging at the corner of the house looks so good to bugs. They fly to it eagerly expecting to enjoy it, I reckon. When the bugs touch the device with that gorgeous light in it, it fries them instantly.

Can we not learn something about appearance *versus* reality from the lesson of the bugs? Is there a message in there about the danger of our embracing inferior quality values?

What is appealing to us and attractive to us might not be good for us. All that seems right to us is not necessarily right for us.

Life is valuing, and it is absolutely vital in the process of coming to grips with the values by which we live our lives to determine which things really are what they purport to be and which ones are not. The value of our values is determined precisely at that point.

What is really worth your energy, your effort, your time, your abilities and your capabilities? Come on now, get down to business on this. What does your heart tell you? It is not quiet about your values, is it? What is important to you? What matters? What do you regard as the excellent things in life? What do you believe is really valuable?

Judgments or opinions about values are not the same as the values themselves. Values are values whether one adheres to them or not. If that is not the case, the values lose their meanings and we are left in a morass of unintelligibility.

Values are like any other propositions, concepts, or beliefs. For them to mean anything, there has to be a way outside of ourselves to test them. If values are relative or situational, such a test becomes impossible.

It is not possible for a thing to be and not to be at the same time and in the same sense. If such were possible, imagine how hopelessly contradictory all that we call truth would become. Inherent in the nature of truth is that it be true in and of itself. Truth cannot contradict itself. Whatever we do with truth does not change what it is.

The same thing is true of values. Abiding values don't change. Read that last sentence one more time.

For me to believe that values are situational or relative demands too much of me intellectually. Why do I say so? Because there is no external, objective standard by which to test the belief. If the value of a value is based upon opinion, there is obviously no objective standard by which it can be tested; therefore, one person's evaluation of a value is no more or less reliable and compelling than another person's evaluation would be.

We have to respect one's freedom to form whatever opinion one wishes, but opinion cannot rationally be used as the measuring rod for truth. If it could, we would have more contradiction than we would know what to do with.

The same line of thought applies to values. There has to be a test for them that goes beyond opinion, otherwise one person's standard is no better nor worse than anyone else's standard. Value standards that are objectively based have an external criterion that is compelling. Value standards that are not objectively based do not have an external criterion, so there is no real way to determine which ones are compelling and which ones are not.

It's all right if you want to criticize me by saying that I am too narrow in my thinking. I do not mind a bit.

For the time being, though, I think I will stay where I am over here in the narrow lane, consoling myself with the thought; *All truth is narrow.* That's why it is truth and not something else. Valuable values do not change. That is why they are so valuable, and that is why the good livers find them so compelling.

Well, that concludes the heavy thinking for now, and I am glad it is over because I am exhausted.

I live a simple life, and things that many folks put a lot of stock in don't mean much to me. There's just a bunch of stuff that I haven't developed much interest in. That's not to say that the things that turn other folks on are not important. To be sure, many of those things are important. I just haven't caught on to 'em yet. I'm not firmly attached to material things. There is too much that is more valuable. I prefer the more basic, simpler, and deeper realities in life.

It's for that reason that it bothers me a bit for folks to take so much interest in money. It's not the valuable value that so many think it is. Money and the quest for it are not the things that make real life come alive. There must be more to it than that. There seem to be a lot of people who have a heap of money who know very little about how life should be lived.

There is nothing wrong with money, *per se.* There is nothing wrong with possessing it. There is something wrong, however, if money possesses people. There is something wrong when folks elevate money to a status that it just does not have. There is something wrong when money is acquired in the wrong way or when it is used as a substitute for character. There is something wrong with believing that possessing money is the purpose of life. There is something wrong when money and what it can buy are sought as the supreme goods in life. These *wrongs* place a value on money that it does not and cannot possibly have. Money is a wonderful possession, but it is a terrible possessor.

Money can buy many things, but not everything. It can buy companions, but not friends. It can buy time in school, but not an education. It can buy a husband or a wife, but not love. It can buy a house, but not a home. It can buy health care, but not health. It can buy convenience, but not character. It can buy things, but not time. It can buy luxury, but not life.

Money cannot buy happiness, nor can it prevent misery. It can buy a mask to create the illusion of happiness, but it cannot buy the real thing.

Have you ever seen a tombstone with the net worth of the deceased chiseled on it? Neither have I. Why is that? It does not matter, I guess, or it would be on there. If it does not matter then, why should it matter so much now? Yet few people can break away from the deadly charm of material abundance. An abundance of material things is not the key to a successful life. The essence that makes life valuable is found elsewhere.

Not only do a lot of folks think that getting money is the most valuable value in life, many of them believe that power is right up at the top on the list of values. To them the valuable is the powerful.

Well, power is valuable. We must have people in the power of authority, and we have to have leaders in government, industry, finance, and business, but power in and of itself is not the answer to the values question.

There are people in positions of power who are not happy because they depend upon their positions to secure happiness for them. Power as an end in itself will make folks as miserable as a woman who was wearing *her sitting down shoes* and her *standing up girdle* at the same time. When is enough power enough?

If neither money nor power can ultimately satisfy us, what's left?

We can always try pleasure. It's a big deal nowadays. Maybe it's the most valuable value around. Perhaps if we just get in on the good times, we will drink deeply enough from the values fountain to be satisfied. But, alas, pleasure fails the value test, too.

Wholesome pleasure is good, mind you, and it's good for us. It is not *the* good, but it is certainly a good. We need some of it, for sure.

Pleasure, any kind of pleasure, as an end in itself is self-defeating and dangerous. Pleasure for its own sake has a way of leaving us empty and unfulfilled. We need recreation and just plain fun to help us recharge our batteries, but pleasure is not the most valuable value in life.

The thing that strikes me most about the values question is that when we try to bring stuff from the outside of us and put it into the inside of us and call it *value*, we are going at it in reverse. Valuable values generate from the inside out, not from the outside in.

Values, principles by which our lives are guided and controlled, should come from the heart, the mind, the control center of life. In terms of values, the heart of the issue is the issue of the heart, the inner essence that makes us what we are. We do things; we strive for things; we think things; we desire things, we believe things because of what we *are*. The heart determines the sort, and the sort, to a remarkable degree, determines the size.

Valuing, then, becomes the hand of the heart. The hand reaches for it if the heart signs off on it. The heart is at the heart of the values question. We need to have our hearts right more than we need to have our problems solved, for our basis determines our behavior.

It is important to remember that whatever values you hold, they are *yours*. Many factors have gone into the formation and development of them, but they are *yours*. You are responsible for your life because it is dictated by *your* values. Remember.

As I was growing up, my parents and some of my teachers tried to teach me about what is really important. Of course, I knew more than any of them did. I didn't pay much attention to them because of inconsistencies I observed between what they were saying and showing and what I was hearing and seeing from my peers and from the *successful* grown folks in my county.

But I grew up, and when I did, I discovered that the more the years jumped on me, the more sense my parents and my teachers had made. They smartened up as time went by. It's amazing how smart they got.

I now know they were right all along. In my younger days, I was too smart to be told any answers and too dumb to know any, but I'm mighty glad I've wised up just a little bit.

It was a significant revelation to learn that the really valuable values in life like happiness, home, character, love for God, country, and family are qualitatively superior to the values that guided so many folks when I was younger and which grip so many people now. My embracing those vital values, the heart kind of values, has redirected, reclaimed, and rechanneled my life, and for that I am forever grateful. What I most cherish is the capacity to appreciate the really valuable values. Knowing the difference helps enormously.

I asked an airline captain, "Why are the big airliners flown at such high altitudes?"

He said, "They operate better when they're up high."

I thought, *So do we humans. We operate better when our values are "up high."*

High quality values produce high quality lives. That's where the good livers operate.

Life is Choosing

Making a decision is sometimes the hardest thing in the world to do, but we have to do it. We have no choice except to choose. Even for us not to make a choice is to make a choice. If we say, "yes," or "no," or "wait," we have made a choice. Making decisions about everything in the book is a constant thing with us. The stuff of life travels on the vehicle of choice.

Thank goodness for our freedom to choose. We are not victims of blind determinism, not merely actors doing what fate has already predestined. We are not the results of a grim fatalism.

A friend told me about a predestinationist who, after falling and breaking his leg, said, "Thank God, that's over."

In order for us to be free and responsible people, we must have choice. We cannot not choose. To be responsible we must be free to choose, and our freedom to choose imposes upon us responsibility for our choices. Neither freedom nor responsibility has meaning unless we have the option to restrict or to release.

Our freedom to choose is an awesome thing. What in the world are you doing with all that freedom?

Obviously then, we have choice, choice about the present and the future. What about the past?

We can't change anything there. Whatever happened at any time before right now is fixed and unrepeatable. It is unique, never to happen again the way it did before. If there were no difference except *when* it happened, that would be enough difference to make it unique and unrepeatable.

We can question the past; we can try to understand it; we can appreciate it or not appreciate it; but we can't change it. The question again: Do we have any choice about the past? Yes, we do. We can choose to study it or not, to learn about it and from it or not. We can look at it scientifically and/or artistically, but learning it and learning from it are all we can do with it. Incidentally, we have done a much better job learning it than we have done learning from it.

We can choose to be informed about the past or to be ignorant of it. One of my college teacher's favorite expressions was, "It's all right to be ignorant, but it's not all right to stay that way." Whichever way we go on that issue, the choice and the consequences are our own.

We have no choice about the past except to learn it and to learn from it, but we do have choice about the present and the future. How does it work? Well, we can choose to change. If we change, both our presents and our futures change too, for our decisions determine our directions.

We can choose to change our attitudes, for attitude is a choice. We can choose to be happy or unhappy, now or at any other time.

Once a doctor said to me, "I wish I could be as happy as you are."

Why am I happy? Because I choose to be. There's not much stuff to *make* me happy; I just am. If you are happy, you are not that way because you have a lot of stuff or because everything is going your way, but because you have chosen to be.

Nothing in the world can make you happy if you don't want to be. Happiness is like education; it's for those who desire it. Happiness? Want it; choose it; you've got it. Is it really that simple? Yes. If choosing to be happy is difficult for anyone, probably the reason for the difficulty lies in its utter simplicity. Folks like for things to be instant, but they don't like for them to be simple, do they?

We can also choose to change how we respond when bad things happen to us. Our lives have their shadows, stresses, and storms. The difference in folks is not that some have their valleys and some don't. It's that some choose to respond to them tragically and some choose to respond to them triumphantly. The present and the future are vitally affected by how we respond to heart-breaking situations.

There are reasons for our choices; they are based on something that goes beyond the thing(s) we choose. They are based on desired outcomes. We choose various kinds of change hoping the change we choose will do for us whatever it is that we want to be done. Obviously we wouldn't choose change if we didn't want something different.

Sometimes change is conditional. This kind of change depends on something or someone else. *I'll change, if . . . .*

I heard a story about a man and his wife who had sixteen children. The family went to a fair where high-quality cattle were being shown.

One cattleman was showing a bull he was especially proud of. He had him in a pen with a curtain drawn all the way around it, and he was charging folks a quarter each to go in and look at his prize bull.

When the man, his wife, and their sixteen children walked up to the pen where the bull was, the daddy asked the owner, "Are you gonna charge me a quarter each for all my family to go in there to see your bull?"

The bull's owner asked, "Are all sixteen of these children yours?"

The daddy said, "Yes, sir, I'm the daddy of every one of 'em."

The cattleman said to the daddy, "I ain't gonna charge y'all nothin', but I'll give you a hundred dollars if you'll go in there and let my bull take a look at you."

That's conditional change.

Change can also be conforming. That's the kind of change folks choose because they want to be like everybody else. The pressure on us to conform is strong, reflecting itself in just about everything that touches our lives, from our appearance to the kinds of vehicles we drive to the way we talk. We struggle with conforming change constantly. It's powerful stuff.

The most important kind of change is compelling change, the kind that is related primarily to personal improvement. It's change that a thoughtful person consents to after careful consideration concerning a course that would be consistent with constructive consequences.

I have experienced compelling change, change that *had* to occur. My need was not interior decoration, but interior transformation. Let me compare it to a house. My need was not new drapes, but new direction; not new lights, but new life; not new furnishings, but a new future; not new carpeting, but new convictions; not new paint, but a new purpose; not a new hearth, but a new heart.

Of course, there is nothing wrong with reformation as far as it goes, but my compulsion was for change that was more than cosmetic, more than rearrangement or remodeling. My need was a new house, not a redone, old one.

Compelling change leads to creative choice. When change compels you, something's going to happen, and relief is just one choice away.

One must be cautious to choose change that brings positive, beneficial results, because we can get clumsy in our choices, and the results can be very bad, causing us to get hurt. It's not pleasant to think about it, but unwise choices can cause crushing change.

My desire at one time in my childhood was to have a tire swing. Other kids had them; there were some at my school, but having one of my own would, I thought, be the icing on my cake.

In our barn there were some short pieces of rope that we used for plow lines. I took three of those short pieces of rope and tied them together to make a rope long enough to reach from a tree limb to the ground.

Managing somehow to get one end of the rope tied to a tree limb, I tied an old tire to the other end of my spliced rope, and, presto, there was my swing.

Near the tree lay a small pile of fence posts. My dad reminded me about them, and he warned me that my swing might not hold me up and that I could fall onto that pile of posts.

What does he know? I thought. *This swing is strong enough to hold up an elephant.*

While I was swinging happily one day, one of the poorly tied knots in the rope came loose and down I went, my head landing smack on the end of one of those fence posts. Bells went off in my head, stars shone brightly, blood flowed, and pain came. A scar, a reminder of my stupid choice, is still with me.

The consequences of my choice were severe enough, but not as much so as they could have been. The experience was enough to instruct me that unwise choices can be crushing, for they have their own, built-in retribution, and their results can be extraordinarily unpleasant.

Just as there are different kinds of change that we can choose, there are also many reasons on the basis of which we choose our changes.

Let me say at the outset that we should beware of choosing to change based on assumption. When we choose a course of action based on an assumption, it seems like a perfectly reasonable thing to do at the time. Don't you feel comfortable when you assume something? Seems to be all right, doesn't it? Most of the time, however, it isn't.

Two of my friends in Louisiana went to the funeral of a man who had achieved prominence in his community, and people came from near and far to the service, so much so that every seat in the church was taken except two seats on the front row in the choir section.

The funeral director asked my friends if they would like to have those two seats. They were thankful that the seats were available, so they took them, preferring to sit there rather than having to stand somewhere else.

During the funeral service, the choir stood to sing; at least my friends thought that, so they concluded that it wouldn't look right for them to remain seated with everyone else in the choir standing, so they stood.

When the music began, they joined in with the singing, thinking that it wouldn't look right for them to just stand there. They related to me that they thought the choir sounded mighty weak, so, as they sang softly, they both eased their heads around slightly and saw that everyone else in the choir section was seated except the two of them and four other people in the front row who composed a quartet singing special music for the service.

Embarrassed beyond all measure, they hastily took their seats.

Making a decision to change something on the basis of assumption can be a drastic mistake.

The farm workers were fascinated with the crop-dusting airplanes that occasionally flew over the fields where they were working. Afraid the planes might crash into them, the workers watched closely any time they came near.

One pilot knew the workers were afraid of the planes, so sometimes he would approach the fields with his prop feathered so that he could fly near the fields as quietly as possible. When he got close to the fields where some workers were, he would change the prop and increase the engine power and head in their direction, nearly scaring the life out of them.

Ronnie McKinney of Cordele, Georgia, told me that he went with his dad to a landing strip where some of the farm workers were loading a plane with sulphur which would be dusted onto a peanut field.

As the workers shoveled the dust into a hopper which carried the sulfur onto the plane, that sulfur dust settled all over them.

After the loading job was completed, four of the workers walked away from the airplane toward their trucks, but one man who was behind them began slapping the dust off his clothes and kicking the ground to get the dust off his rubber boots.

Two of the farm workers in front of him assumed that all that slapping and kicking behind them was the racket of the plane's engine starting up, and they began running hard toward their trucks. The two immediately behind them saw them, and they took off running, too.

None of the four had a good reason to run, but the two in front later said they ran because they were afraid the plane was starting up and might *get them* and the other two said they ran just because they saw the other two running.

Whether it results in embarrassment, brings about hilarious results or precipitates a really serious situation, making a choice on the basis of an assumption is not the wisest thing for us to do.

Making decisions based on the advice of other people is not always wise either, especially if it's a spur-of-the-moment decision.

During the first service of a revival meeting in a small country church, the guest preacher said to the congregation, "If there is anybody here who really wants this church to have a revival, and, if you would be willing for God to take your life if that's what it would take for this church to have a revival, come down here to the altar and pray for God to take your life."

The fellow telling me this story said he asked the man seated next to him if he was going down to the altar and pray that prayer.

The man answered, "No, I ain't goin' to do it. I *believe* in prayer."

I like his decision better than I like the preacher's advice, don't you?

Change is choice and choice is change. A most significant thing about our lives is that to a remarkable degree they are results of our choices. Sort of sobering, isn't it? The choices are yours and mine; we call the shots, and we live with the score.

The good livers choose to choose wisely.

Life is Learning

The one thing I have definitely learned in life is that I don't know very much about anything, but I do know that the more I have ever learned, the more I learned that I had not learned enough. It's better that way. The more any thinking person knows, the more that person knows that more is to be known. Learning is never-ending; school is never out for one who yearns to live excellently.

I am afraid of people who have learned so much that they know everything. Have you ever known folks like that? Know-it-alls? No matter what the questions are, they know the answers? No matter what the problems are, they know the solutions? No matter what the subject is, they know how to discuss it? Folks like that bother the heck out of me. They break me out in a rash. Something is wrong with people who are always right.

In a graduate seminar, a student asked a professor a question that for all practical purposes was unanswerable. Any answer would have been utter speculation or conjecture. The professor wisely replied, "I do not know."

The silly student saw an opportunity to let his knowledge enrapture the entire class as well as the professor whose scholarship the student obviously thought needed some help. Totally dissatisfied with the professor's response, the student proceeded to answer his own question. *This will impress everybody in here*, the student must have been thinking.

The professor, allowing the student to go on for about five minutes, interrupted and said, "Sir, I did not say that *you* do not know. I said that *I* do not know."

The student suddenly got lockjaw. It became eerily quiet in the room.

I learned something important that day, and it has served me well in my adult life. If one is a *know-it-all*, it's better for that person to keep that hyper-learning to himself and just enjoy all that knowledge in private. Some folks say more by being quiet than they do by talking. Sometimes the loudest know the least. How important it is to give the tongue a lot of time off. Little minds and big mouths keep close company.

Quietness and teachability are mighty admirable qualities. Humility is always a prime requisite for any learning that matters. It's important to be open-minded; it's more important not to let your brain fall out.

When asked about the key to his success, an industrialist said, "Knowledge. I have to adjust as my knowledge permits. I can do no more than I know."

Isn't that good?

There is no premium on ignorance, and there is no more rational act than to know to do what you know how to do. To do otherwise can create a swarm of problems.

I expected that industrialist to give me an involved discussion about business practice, about technology and its applications, about marketing, about total quality management, about employer-employee relations, about something besides what he told me. I was impressed by the brevity and the simplicity, and, yes, the power of his answer. It's so good and rewarding to be quite quiet and benefit from the words of the wise.

Everything that man of manufacturing does is captured in his answer, and his response cut to the heart of the matter. Knowledge is power.

If you want to do more, learn more. That's what he meant. If you want to learn, be open to new, fresh ideas and approaches. That principle applies to excellence in anything from carpentry to cooking. We learn more by doing things than we learned when we were learning how to do them. Learning to be a learner is a priceless lesson. It's one of life's most important lessons.

Some of what I've learned along the way I can use. Some I can't. If I can, I do. If I can't, I don't. In either case, I don't complain that I had to learn things that are of no use to me now. Whether I can use the knowledge and skills I have picked up, I have had a heck of a good time learning the dab I have learned.

When I was in school, I wanted to get everything the teacher taught. If the teacher thought it was important enough to teach, I thought it was important enough to learn. I could sort out later what could be used in my life and what couldn't. The important thing in school for me was to suspend any notions about the future utility of the material and try to learn the material or the skill. All of it. Perhaps my goal was unrealistic, but I couldn't imagine the teacher teaching something that I was not supposed to learn.

Think about it. Can you imagine a teacher saying, "I want to teach you about punctuation, but you don't have to learn what I'm teaching about the use of commas?"

What if a medical school professor were to say to the students, "All this material we have discussed today you need to know except the part about the diseases of the ear."

What about a law professor saying to the students, "You do not have to learn the material about contract law."

What would you think of a dental professor who told the students, "Be sure to learn all the procedures we have been through except the one about tooth extraction."

My goodness, Wayne, you may be thinking, *you know that in education there are some things that are more important than others. Why not stress the important and let the minor things slide?*

All right. If it's important, teach it and expect the students to learn it. If it's not important, leave it alone. That's my answer. Why in the world would a teacher teach the unimportant? Teachers should know their materials well enough to know what's important and what isn't.

We might as well learn what is taught. If it's worth teaching, it's worth learning. In learning, it's important to be comprehensive. We can decide later what to do with the learning. For the time being, learn it.

One way I learn is by asking questions. It is not my intention to irritate folks, but I love to ask questions of informed people, and I will if the opportunity comes along.

I was talking to a farmer about different crops. I asked him, "What brand of hybrid corn yields best?"

He said, "I really don't know."

I asked, "What's the optimum average temperature for growing soybeans?"

He said, "You got me there. I don't know about that."

I tried one more time. "What variety of wheat is best suited for our area of the country?"

He said, "I declare I don't know. I'll have to look it up."

I said, "I hope you don't mind my questions."

He said, "I don't mind a bit. How else can you learn anything if you don't ask questions?"

I don't know. How?

The guy at the same table where all of the guests at a banquet were seated was a physics teacher. I couldn't resist.

"What is electricity?" I asked him, and I really wanted to know.

When he finished answering me, I said to him kiddingly, "You don't know what it is either, do you?"

He took it well, thank goodness. He backed up, got off the textbook talk and simplified his answer for me. He illustrated it with a mental picture of water flowing through a hose so that I could understand the ideas of flow and pressure. That helped considerably.

I still don't know exactly what electricity is, but I know more than before. I even understand *volt* and *amp* a little more clearly.

A friend of mine is an internal medicine specialist. I've heard about that medical specialty for a while, but I didn't know what was meant by *internal medicine*. I thought it was the opposite of *external medicine*. Anyway, I asked my friend to explain it to me.

He said, "An internal medicine specialist is the same thing to adults that a pediatrician is to children and adolescents."

Now I know.

An appropriate question of an appropriate person at an appropriate time is appropriate, don't you think? A lot of worthwhile knowledge is acquired like that.

We learn in all kinds of ways. Adversity, for example, is an excellent teacher. Sometimes learning comes painfully. Suffering, sorrow, pain, agony, heartache, trouble, and trial are part and parcel of life. Most of us can't escape some or all of them. Life at times can be a rough, rugged terrain.

Adversities are not all bad, though, because we can learn some of life's most important lessons in the midst of adversity, learning things that we could not or would not learn any other way.

Having been involved in a horrible accident several years ago, I know a little bit about the learning value of adversity.

Before that accident, I had a major ego problem. Learning something about myself as a result of that accident, and learning that life is mighty uncertain, and learning that the world and everybody in it could get along without me were much-needed revelations. My life now is one of those *before and after* deals. Upon reflection on what I thought about myself before the wreck and what I think about myself now, I have come to the conclusion that there is no comparison between me *before* and me *after*. There is only contrast, thank God.

Adversity is a super teacher. This conviction will always abide in my consciousness: If something drastic had not happened to me, there would have been no change in me. There is hardly any reason for adversity if it doesn't teach us.

Some of our learning might not come painfully, but it causes pain because we learn things about ourselves that are painful. Self-recognition can sometimes be a real jolt. Have you ever learned something about yourself that caused you to say, "I didn't realize I was that way?" I expect we all have. It's painful, but it's helpful because now we can make adjustments. Now we can make corrections. Now we know better. This kind of self-awareness learning makes us more accountable and more responsible.

I used to tell jokes on people in audiences without first asking them if they would mind.

A man in one audience did not appreciate my joking about him, and he made his feelings about his lack of appreciation exceedingly clear. That he reacted the way he did toward me taught me an important lesson. Now I don't *pick on* anyone in any audience unless the person tells me that it will be all right. Now I know better.

Knowledge that opens understanding to us, that improves our skills, that helps us relate to people more intelligently, that helps us to understand ourselves more clearly, and that nourishes our minds and broadens our horizons is quite legitimate, and we should seek it eagerly. Good livers are invariably good learners.

I believe in formal education with all my heart. Its value can be enormous. Formal education exposes one to ideas that stretch the mind, helps one to develop reasoning abilities, and it stresses individual responsibility. Doing the formal education thing is something I'm glad I got in on.

As great as formal education is, life education, learning lessons that are not academically structured, is absolutely important, too. Once we have knowledge, we need to know what to do with it. Knowing what to do with what we know is called wisdom. A bucket of that is worth it all, isn't it? Common sense coupled with formal education are a beautiful complement to each other.

Along with acquiring information or some sort of skill, we need to learn how to think, how to apply, how to relate. Learning should help us to become wise and humble, wise so that we can understand and humble so that we will not be arrogant.

Learning should dispel arrogance as it dispels ignorance. An educated mind coupled with an uneducated heart creates more problems than it solves. Why can't we have bright heads and bright hearts? Wouldn't that combination work out all right? It's wise to get a heart full of sensitivity to go along with a head full of sense. An informed mind and an illuminated heart go together beautifully. Education and foolishness don't match up well.

Diction along with decency are a winning team.
Grammar along with goodness are a great pair.
Syntax along with sagacity are bright sunshine.
Science along with service are mankind's glory.
Mathematics along with manners are a real plus.
Literature along with love are an ideal couple.
Reading along with reason are a beautiful symmetry.
Writing along with wisdom form a captivating excellence.
History along with hope are the heart and soul of humanity.
Medicine along with mercy are the essence of godliness.
Music along with magnanimity are a harmonious duet.
Geography along with generosity are an eloquent language.
Economics along with encouragement are a priceless tapestry.
Psychology along with purity are wisdom's counselor.
Religion along with reality are an irresistible sermon.

Learning is the lesson, knowledge is the key, and wisdom is the way to an intelligent, informed, and involved life.

The good livers' class is always in session. I wonder who the next student will be?

Life is Loving

There are alternatives to love, but there is no substitute for it and there is no equivalent to it. Love is in a special class all its own.

The extent to which you qualify as a good liver can best be measured by determining the reality, the depth, the quality, and the extent of your love. All other human qualities taken together without love leave a void within us that cannot be filled.

Love is our source of stability and happiness, giving us the balance that we need so much, creating within us the sense that we are, in fact, a part of real life. If we are not a part, we will come apart, won't we? Love wonderfully and even miraculously prevents apartness and in the same ways creates belonging. There is no joy in life without love. Love, therefore, is the key to human well-being and happiness.

Love comes from within us. Whatever we might do externally, be it ever so worthy of the applause of others, doesn't amount to much if we are motivated to do it by some other force besides love. Human acts not motivated by love amount to zero. If love is not the reason for the deed, the deed in and of itself is just a loud noise.

We are capable of some very significant, even heroic acts and achievements, but for them to be really valuable where it counts, they must be motivated by love. Such motivation comes from within us. Love is the most powerful motivator in the world.

If we have love, we will demonstrate it, for love is a practical and obvious thing. It starts on the inside, but in the demonstration of its reality, it is made evident externally. Love always lets itself be known. It doesn't have something to prove, but it always proves itself. We can't keep our love bottled up or hidden, for if it's in there, it will show itself out here. Love doesn't sit around doing nothing. It is active, not passive. Love is not a subject for argument, but for action. It's demonstrable. Love is an action word. *Love* is a verb.

On their wedding day, a groom said to his bride, "I want you to know that I love you, and, if I ever change my mind, I'll let you know."

Sounds crude and abrupt, doesn't it?

Perhaps this is the interpretation: "I love you, and I'll *show* you that I love you. I might not be saying it to you, but the way I treat you will prove my love for you. You won't doubt the evidence."

I doubt that she ever had reason to doubt his love for her.

Wives like to hear the words, *I love you*, from their husbands and, of course, it's nice, I reckon; but I'll bet you in the final analysis they would rather know love from their husbands by demonstration than by declaration. I suppose husbands like to hear, *I love you*, from their wives too. It's not a one-way street, right? Whoever says it to whom is not the pivotal thing here. The important thing is that action is better than announcement, and proof is more credible than a profession.

Words are cheap. They are sometimes used as a substitute for practical love. Not all the time, mind you, but sometimes. It's so easy to say; it's incalculably precious to show. Where love really resides; not merely in words, but in reality, there will follow an expression of it.

Love reveals itself in many ways. We cannot define love. I know I can't. Can you? I guess no one really knows how to define it precisely. So what? Love is better experienced than defined, It's one of those things that we know we have or don't have; we're just not quite certain what it is.

A deacon said to his preacher, "I'm praying for you to get the unction."

The preacher asked, "Praying for me to get the unction? What in the world is that?"

The deacon answered, "I don't know exactly, but I know you ain't got it."

That's the way love is. You might not know exactly what it is, but you know whether you've got it.

All right, so we can't define love exactly. We can demonstrate it, and that's the important thing anyway. That's what matters. Most folks I know are too busy for definitions anyway. They just want to see things done, not defined. I don't blame them for that. Obviously definitions are helpful, but life consists not in defining, but in doing. Things are what they are no matter what their names are. It doesn't really matter that we can't put the meaning of the word *love* into words; we can put it into our ways. Manners mean more than meanings. We love; therefore, we show it. We don't love so that we can hoard it, but so that we can give it away, thus proving that it's real. Love's reality in us is love's authority over us. Read that last sentence again.

If you can't give love, you don't have love, and, consequently, you can't accept love. It's difficult if not impossible for you to accept what you are unable or unwilling to give. If you have love, you give love so that you can keep love in order to give it again. You can't give your love away to the extent that you have less left, for the more of your love you give, the more you have. Keep on giving love so that you can get more love so you'll have more of it to give which creates more room for you to receive the love that comes back to you. Love multiplies itself over and over the more it's given.

Love is made evident in many ways. There are some things that love is, and there are some things love is not. Love is courteous; it is not crude, There are some things that love does and some things it doesn't do. Love inspires; it doesn't insult.

Love can't be explained, but it can be described. The descriptions that follow are not the textbook type, not technical, not academic, not erudite. They should be useful to us, then, shouldn't they? They are not exhaustive, Lord knows, but maybe they're representative enough.

Love is helpfully described by the term *acceptance*.

Love doesn't demand terms or set limits. It's unconditional. Love doesn't say, *I'll accept you if you'll clean up*. It says, *I accept you. Now clean up*.

Love doesn't say, *I love you because you deserve it*. All of us have imperfections, flaws and sins, but they don't make us unworthy of being loved. If our shortcomings made us unworthy of love, we would all be in a mess because none of us could measure up. Who among us deserves to be loved? To say that we deserve love would be like saying that we deserve mercy. Merit and mercy are not the same. Merit is deserved; mercy isn't. Love doesn't love folks on the basis of merit or worthiness. It loves them for who they are. Folks who really love don't pick and choose whom to love and whom not to love. People are worth loving, their unworthiness notwithstanding. Love accepts folks, flaws and all. The cleaning up can come later, and it should. There might be a lot of it needing to be done, but it can be done later. For the time being, love or acceptance is enough.

A vital cog in the acceptance wheel is an unwillingness to being party to censorious, fault-finding criticism of other folks. Love soars above that sorry enterprise. The one who loves tries to help people, not abuse them. You can't make yourself look better by trying to make someone else look bad. Most of the faults you criticize in others are the faults that you are most aware of in your own life.

Dreaming up negative things to say about people, censorious criticism, gossip, or anything kin to those kinds of pathetic involvements is never designed to help anyone; it is unkind; it is worthless, and it is packed with potential dangers. Think about this: If one will engage in gossipy discussions with you concerning someone else, that person will also engage in gossipy discussions with someone else about you.

It's not corny. Love looks for ways to help folks, not to hurt them. It looks for ways to develop folks, not to demolish them. It looks for ways to inspire folks, not to injure them. Love looks for the good in folks. There's some there, and love finds it.

Besides acceptance, another appropriate description of love is *forgiveness*.

The two greatest needs we humans have are love and forgiveness. We need to receive both, and we need to offer both.

One of our most difficult tasks in life is to forgive someone who has hurt us. Most folks had rather *get 'em back* than to forgive them. Pride is our worst enemy when we get down to this forgiveness thing. A lot of people prefer to hold on to their stubborn pride than to give in and do all they can to repair ruptured relationships.

Resentment harbored and an unwillingness to forgive can cause immeasurable damage. We need to forgive as we need forgiveness, and in order for us to be forgiven, we have to forgive. The one who will not forgive will not be forgiven because that person is not forgivable. For me to call such a condition *profound* would be a monumental understatement.

A lady said to me, "I'll never forgive my parents for what they did to me."

I've heard things like, "I'll forgive, yeah, when hell freezes over," or, "I'd love to knock the devil out of 'em, but I ain't about to forgive 'em."

The most hate-filled laughter I ever heard came from a man when I suggested that he forgive his wife for the way she treated him. I'll never forget that laugh. It sent chills down my spine; it numbed my soul with fear.

Forgiveness is a rare commodity nowadays. That's why it's so precious.

Two men in the same community had a long-standing grudge going on between them. Their mutual bitterness kept them from speaking to each other for over thirty years.

One of them became very ill, and it looked like he wasn't going to pull through.

In light of that development, the other fellow decided he had better try to get things straightened out before it was too late. He went over to the sick man's place to see about patching things up.

It was a tense meeting at first, but after a while, it looked like the two were actually going to bury the hatchet.

They went so far as to shake hands on it.

When the visitor headed for the door, the sick one said, "Look here, now, if I get well, the old grudge still holds."

It's difficult to forgive, isn't it? Yes, but it's certainly much more difficult not to.

About thirty years ago I became acquainted with him. To be quite honest and plain about it, I couldn't stand him.

My negative feelings toward him grew more and more intense. I had never known before what it meant to hate someone, that is, I had not experienced it personally. I wasn't sure what it felt like, but I was beginning to feel for that fellow what I thought was hatred. It was somewhat frustrating for me because I didn't know how I was supposed to treat someone I hated. The only way I knew how to handle the situation was to ignore him. After all, the supreme insult is to ignore, isn't it? That's what I did, but it didn't help. My ill will toward him began to get to me. Filled with animosity toward him to the extent that it was affecting my sleep, I would wake up during the night thinking of all sorts of bad things that I hoped would happen to him. Horrible feelings toward him when someone mentioned his name made me tremble inside. I was in a mess, and it was getting worse.

Harboring viciously negative feelings toward him for about two years was the worst experience I have ever forced upon myself; it was the worst period that I have ever known.

Being much younger then and being infinitely more stupid, it took a while for me to come to my senses. It finally dawned on me that I was doing enormous damage to myself. Thinking about virtually nothing else than how much I despised him was tearing me apart. That foolishness had to stop.

Realizing that if ever there was going to be peace within me again, I *had* to ask for his forgiveness. The problem had to be resolved. It just wouldn't do to let it continue. I wanted so much to come clean with him. I wanted him to know how I felt, what I had been going through, and how much I wanted it to stop. He already knew all about my feelings, but I wanted to tell him man to man. Nothing else, I was convinced, would stop the madness.

Going to his home to ask for his forgiveness, to beg if I had to, was the most difficult thing I have ever done, but there was no other way to deal with a problem that was eating my heart out of me.

I poured out everything I was feeling and had felt regarding him, confessing to him as honestly and as plainly as I could. I talked to him about the results of my hating him.

He listened graciously, extremely graciously.

When I had said all I could think of to say, he said something that shook me to the foundations of my being.

He said, "Wayne, I have already forgiven you. I'm glad, though, that you came to talk to me because I want to tell you that even though I had forgiven you before you asked me to, I never would have respected you if you had not talked to me about this unfortunate situation. You had my forgiveness before you asked for it. Now you have my respect, too."

I had no idea that he would respond like that. I was absolutely overwhelmed. I was already forgiven! In his heart he had already done it! Besides that, now he respected me!

After that visit, I felt as though the weight of the earth had been lifted off me. I could relax now, sleep now, enjoy my life now, do some creative work now.

That man taught me a lesson I will never forget. He loved unconditionally; therefore, he forgave me. What a lesson! What a man he was!

Love and forgiveness are not just words, they're realities. Love is forgiveness; forgiveness is love. We need to receive both; we need to offer both.

Love's many-faceted description not only includes acceptance and forgiveness, it also includes *helpfulness*.

Love doesn't merely refrain from harming, it rejoices in helping. I've heard some folks say, "If we can't help people, we certainly won't harm them." Perhaps that is said without the awareness that sometimes the most severe harm is not to help.

Not to help people who refuse help is one thing. No one can help in those cases. Not to help people who need, want, and would welcome help is another matter. There is a world of difference between unwanted and ungiven help.

Helpfulness comes clothed in many and various garbs. It might be friendship; or encouragement; or time; or a listening, sympathetic ear; or a visit; or *just being there;* or volunteer service; or assisting in emergencies. There are multitudes of ways to help people. Love looks for those ways. You can count on love to find ways to be counted on.

Love is helpfulness, giving itself away on behalf of others.

The happiest people have learned that the fundamentally important thing in life is giving, not getting. They are of more value to themselves and to others because that lesson has sunk in. They have learned that it is better to bask in the sunshine of generosity and service and helpfulness than it is to rot in the dank, dark dungeon of selfishness. They have learned that the rewards of getting are infinitesimal, but the rewards of giving are infinite. They have learned that they are not on this earth to be reservoirs, but they are here to be fresh, ever-flowing streams. They have been helped; therefore, they help. They have been given to; therefore, they give. They have learned that giving creates the capacity to receive, for they cannot receive into fullness; they receive into emptiness. They have learned that not giving takes the fun out of getting.

Love has taught them that it is the giving spirit that lifts life to the heights. Giving is the artist's brush that strokes people with a strength and beauty unique to those who are engaged in the fine art of living life excellently. Giving is an expression of a heart that is sensitive enough to be tender, selfless enough to be kind, compassionate enough to be gracious, and generous enough to be limitless.

The good livers help themselves most by helping others. I don't understand the paradox, but it's clear to me, nonetheless, that the more we give, the more we have. It works out that way every time. The more love we give, the more love we have to give. The more time we give, the more time we seem to have to give. When we really want something done, we get someone who is busy, for it appears that the people who give time are the ones who have time. The more happiness we give, the more happiness we have. The more services we render, the more capable we become to render the services and the more opportunities will present themselves for us to render those services.

Love helpfully gives itself away on behalf of others.

Another apt description of love is *unselfishness*. Whatever selfishness is, love is not; whatever love is, selfishness is not.

The emptiest kind of fullness is to be full of oneself. Selfishness and love cannot occupy the same life at the same time. For us to be healthy, we have to love ourselves; but I'm not talking about self-love, I'm talking about selfishness, and they are not synonymous. Self-love is all right; selfishness is all wrong. You can love yourself without being full of yourself, but you cannot be selfish without being self-full.

Whatever is wrong with people is caused by selfishness. It is at the root of all human problems and mistakes. Selfish people become stunted in their spirits and darkened in their souls because they have little or no interest in the really important things in life. Selfishness is the ultimate form of conceit. Selfish folks measure every event, every relationship and every transaction in terms of what they can get out of it for themselves. Selfishness generates suspicion and misery. It is an extraordinarily powerful, degenerative force having the capacity to destroy the very purpose of one's existence. It is the supreme enemy of life, causing life to have an unlimited narrowness.

The self-giving, self-sacrificing spirit that real love produces is alien to and rises above the attitudes about life that most folks seem to have nowadays. When it comes to giving or getting, most people will take getting every time, preferring being served to serving; preferring having to giving. It has always been trendy to be selfish, but it has never worked. A self-centered, self-serving spirit makes life miserably unhappy. It always has; it always will. There is no way to justify a selfish life.

Selfishness never wins. People are lauded, applauded, appreciated, revered, memorialized, and held in high esteem for what they give, not what they get.

For folks to be selfish is for them to miss life. What selfish people have is a cheap imitation of the real thing. The real thing, real life, does exist. Some try to counterfeit the real thing, and by doing so give evidence to the fact that the real thing exists, for no one tries to counterfeit something that does not exist. Selfish people try to make a substitution for the genuine article, authentic life, by going through a process of getting in order to keep. That's only a pose, dramatics; it misses reality. They grab at life, but it eludes them because they attempt to live life in reverse, writing their scripts from the outside in rather than from the inside out. The unfortunate drama has a miserable outcome, however, for, no matter how cleverly they manipulate the plot, they can't resolve the fundamental problem because the problem has no resolution other than a reversal of the point of origin. The core determines the course. Selfishness starts wrong, stays wrong, and concludes wrong.

The problem facing selfish people is one of perspective and belief from which their points of view are framed. If they really believe that it's possible for them to live life fully and authentically and to be selfish at the same time, they're operating in a fantasy world. It's an illusion. The attempt is a miserable exercise in futility because it doesn't conform to reality.

Love and selfishness come from different sources; they follow different routes and they arrive at different destinations.

Another beautiful description of love is *courtesy*.

Courtesy is love expressed in little things, and, you know, there are many more of them in life than there are big ones. Have you ever noticed how big life is in little things? How many there are of them? It follows, then, if life consists mostly of little things, we can cover a lot of ground by expressing our love in them.

A man told me that when he and his wife married forty years ago, he told her he would take care of all the major matters if she would handle all the minor ones. "She agreed," he said, "and, so far, there have been no major matters."

Love is sensitive to life's little things. The kiss for the spouse as you leave home is a little thing, but it's an important thing. I've heard that men who regularly do that will live longer than those who don't, so, men, it's worth it even if you don't like her. Just kidding, ladies.

Courtesy is love in little things. A sincere compliment is a big little thing. *Thank you* is a big little thing. A pleasant smile, a kind word, a reassuring word, an understanding word, gentleness, respect, all those are big little things. They are courtesy; they are love. Courtesy is polite and mannerly. Above all, it's careful not to offend anyone. Little things are important too. Who among us can measure the importance of love expressed in life's little things?

Love is characterized by acceptance, forgiveness, helpfulness, unselfishness, and courtesy; moreover, it is characterized by humility.

Love is always humble. Humility is meekness, not weakness. It is strength that is under control, strength that is gentle, but it *is* strength. It is strength with a harness on it.

Love is humble. It is not boastfully pride-filled. Pride is a good thing if it motivates you to do excellent work, to be your best, to be clean and neat. There is nothing wrong with that kind of pride. Pride is a bad thing, however, if it leads you to be arrogant or haughty, or if it causes you to think that you are inherently *better* than other folks. Arrogance is always ugly, and it is one thing that love never produces in anybody. Love and boastful pride cannot live together peacefully.

Love does not push itself. It does not seek self-glorification. It does not submit tamely to abuse, to be sure, but it is gentle and easy-going. Humility is a tender toughness in whose house love happily dwells.

Another expression of the many facets of love is patience, the willingness to wait for a desired result in yourself or in others.

It's rare to see patience practiced nowadays. We live in a hurry-up world, preferring instant stuff: instant food, instant information, instant results. Patience is a fading art form, not fitting our busy lifestyle very well. How much we have lost because we don't take time for it!

Love is great for its patience, not inclined to hurry except in an emergency, but taking time for the important: people in need, the sick and the dying, the distressed, the burdened, the lonely, the elderly, the children, the disabled, the troubled. Love takes the time to demonstrate that it's worthy of its name.

Love expresses itself in acceptance, forgiveness, helpfulness, unselfishness, courtesy, humility, and patience.

Whatever uplifting qualities there are in life, love fosters and sustains them.

Love is a magnificent quality not only in what it favors for us but also in what it opposes for us, favoring what is good and right and opposing what is bad and wrong.

Love favors accord; it opposes anger.

Love favors benevolence; it opposes badness.
Love favors compassion; it opposes censoriousness.
Love favors discipline; it opposes dissonance.
Love favors encouragement; it opposes egoism.
Love favors forgiveness; it opposes flippancy.
Love favors genuineness; it opposes gall.
Love favors helpfulness; it opposes hostility.
Love favors initiative; it opposes indolence.
Love favors joy; it opposes jealousy.
Love favors kindness; it opposes knavery.
Love favors liberty; it opposes licentiousness.
Love favors manners; it opposes malevolence.
Love favors nurture; it opposes nastiness.
Love favors opportunity; it opposes oppression.
Love favors patience; it opposes perfidy.
Love favors quality; it opposes quarrelsomeness.
Love favors reasonableness; it opposes rudeness.
Love favors simplicity; it opposes snobbishness.
Love favors tact; it opposes turbulence.
Love favors understanding; it opposes umbrage.
Love favors virtue; it opposes vice.
Love favors wisdom; it opposes wickedness.

Love in action speaks far more eloquently than any words can ever tell. The extent to which you love is the extent to which you live. There are many keys to a successful, significant, purposeful, and peaceful life, but the greatest of these keys is love.

Conclusion

A minister preached the same sermon *verbatim* for four successive Sundays.

Having grown tired of it, one of the members of the congregation asked the preacher, "Why do you preach the same sermon over and over?"

The minister replied, "When y'all start practicing this sermon, I'll preach a different one."

Thinking about and talking about worthwhile ideas and beliefs is good. To practice them is even better. Now that you have read this book, you are wiser. If you practice what you have read, you will be happier.

You should neither be threatened nor frightened by life, but you should get hold of it without fear or hesitation, for, if you don't, it will throw you around mercilessly. You can't merely lay hold of life, you must let it lay hold of you.

To achieve the status of good livers, you and I have to apply the qualities of life in a harmonious balance, for the key to a wiser, happier life is balance because balance blends the various elements contributing to excellent living into a healthy control center from which the issues of real life proceed. Living *from* a center of principles is better than living *by* a list of rules. Living from a balanced center, that's the way to go.

You can be able without being boastful.
You can be bold without being foolish.
You can be confident without being arrogant.
You can be a dreamer without being visionary.
You can be efficient without being mechanical.
You can be frank without being insulting.
You can be gentle without being weak.
You can be happy without being shallow.
You can be informed without being garrulous.
You can be just without being judgmental.
You can be kind without being condescending.
You can be light-hearted without being silly.
You can be mannerly without being manipulative.
You can be neighborly without being nosy.
You can be optimistic without being unrealistic.
You can be pure without being austere.
You can be quiet without being placid.
You can be reserved without being unfriendly.
You can be sensitive without being spineless.

You can be tough-minded without being stubborn.

You can be useful without being sedulous.

You can be victorious without being domineering.

You can be witty without being caustic.

You can be youthful without being impulsive.

You can be zestful without being fanatical.

In short, you can be balanced.

Life from the center. Try a healthy balance that keeps everything in perspective. Pretty soon you'll get used to it, and you'll learn to like it.

Life. What a thrilling adventure!

Let's get on with it.